Aiming for the Heart

ISBN: 978-1-937720-53-7

Sea Hill Press Inc.

SEA·HILL
PRESS

www.seahillpress.com

Aiming for the Heart

A Novel
by BARBARA KEATING

The world breaks every one and afterward many are strong at the broken places.

—Ernest Hemingway, *A Farewell to Arms*

Chapter

One

The late November sun shone brightly through the hospital window. Kate stared toward the view of the blue sky, shivered and wondered if it was as cold out there as she felt in her soul this morning.

"I circled that parking lot looking for a place to park, Kate. I would have been here sooner. I came as soon as I heard from your mom," Liz Van Allen said, a determined, nervous look on her round face. She sat close to Kate, holding her hand and looking attentively into the bleary eyes of her closest friend. Liz's voice stayed low and serious, accentuating the somber atmosphere in this room at Marshall Memorial Hospital. "You put up a good front last night, Kate. Now tell me what's really been going on."

Kate felt weak and ashamed after yesterday's terrifying events. The traumatic, seemingly endless hours of the previous night continued to work on her mind.

As the two friends sat in the hospital room, Liz's hands began to involuntarily shake. Seeing Kate looking so despondent, Liz's usual calm deserted her. Liz was always the one everybody depended on. Maybe it came with her five-foot ten-inch height and large body frame. Her dark brown hair looked like a frayed mop today. No time to blow it dry before setting out on this latest rescue mission.

Liz had always envied Kate, who had seemed to have it all. Kate was five foot five, slender yet curvy, almost delicate. Her straight, light brown hair fell to her shoulders, and her green eyes sparkled. How much pain those eyes hid, Liz realized.

To hide her anxiety from Kate, Liz got up from the bed and opened the hospital blinds. "Damn these windows. You'd think they would open and let in some fresh air, for God's sake."

Liz shook her full head of dark, curly hair. Kate's mind flashed on the prior evening's hours spent with Liz before the ugly, unexpected action unfolded . . .

The snow fell fast, fast, at eight thirty last night when Kate Parker had first called Liz.

"I can't stop pacing," Kate said to Liz. "The night is just stretching so long ahead of me. The silence is driving me crazy."

Liz felt the anxiety in her friend's voice. "How about I come over so we can go crazy together? I've been dying to tell you what happened to me today. You won't believe it."

"What happened?" Kate said.

"I'll come around if that's okay. I'd love to get out of the house. Mitch just got back from giving a talk at a conference, and I really don't feel like listening to a blow-by-blow account of how great his psych talk was."

"Okay. I'll check on the boys and light a fire. See you soon."

Twenty minutes later, a gust of cold air whooshed in behind Liz. Rubbing her cold hands, she smiled at her friend, who had been pacing the rug. They hugged hello and went into the living room.

"Eric left some Mai Tai mix in the liquor cabinet before I threw him out," Kate said. "How does that sound? We can pretend it's a tropical evening and we're drinking in Hawaii instead of freezing our asses off in Stony Brook."

"Why not? Let's have a few!"

They both giggled at the thought. Two bad girls together.

"I'll be back in a few minutes. I need to read the package directions," Kate said.

Kate soon returned with two glasses filled to their brims.

"These look dangerous." Liz laughed, looking at the tall glasses.

"Nah. What's the problem? The kids are asleep, and we're big girls!"

They talked and got comfortable, and before long they had downed one and were onto their second. The fire was going full force. Kate lay down next to Winnie, their terrier pup, on the rug before the fireplace.

"Aren't we lucky, with all the Earth Day goody-goodies everywhere, that we can still throw some real wood logs on and enjoy a couple of relaxing forbidden fruits?" Kate joked. "It's good to live on Eastern Long Island after all, freezing cold or not." After another pop of her drink, Kate turned her head to look up at Liz. "So, tell me what happened to you today."

Liz hesitated a bit, thought for a moment, and then started telling Kate about her experience that day at their local garage. "Well, I decided not to be one of those helpless women who get their cars fixed but don't understand anything about repairs themselves. So, I made an appointment over at Ron's Mobil Garage to get a tune up and learn a few things, so I wouldn't feel dumb." Liz twisted her fingers in her hair, speaking in a soft rush of words.

Kate asked, "So, what did you learn?"

Liz was silent for a few moments, then said, "Well, . . . Ron opened the hood. I was looking into the engine, when he grabs me from behind, leans over me and . . ."

"And?"

Liz's face reddened. "Well, suddenly, Ron starts feeling me up!"

Kate's face fell. "I take my car there all the time. I never figured him for a creep, just a dull, robotic sort of guy. What an asshole! This is as gross as the assholes in Hollywood who think they can get away with anything for the promise of an acting job."

"Now I don't know what to do." Liz groaned. "What do I say to Mitch when it's time to take the car in for repairs? I just don't know how to handle it. I never want to go back to Ron's garage, but

Mitch thinks he does great repairs. Plus, Ron's work is cheap, and you know how Mitch loves a bargain."

"We'll think of something, like Ron kept you waiting too long for parts, or he overcharged you."

Kate was already feeling the depressing effect of the Mai Tais. After supper, she had taken an Ativan for anxiety. Just thinking about her bitter divorce proceedings with Eric had her jumpy. All day long she alternated between anxiety and depression—alternately, her heart would pound and her mood would sink. After she had put the boys into bed, she decided one more pill would ease her jitters. So, before Liz arrived, Kate downed another Ativan.

Now she could hear Liz talking dimly, but her own thoughts raced crazily, drowning out Liz's words. *My separation is not even a month old, and I feel my energy and spirit flagging so much. And here I was the one who ended the marriage. What a joke! I hate Eric coming over to pick up the boys, throwing all his conquests in my face. He didn't want to leave at first. Now he's talking bullshit, riding the crest of a carefree bachelor again, throwing it in my face all the time. Why do I take it? Maybe I'm the crazy one.*

"Kate, what do you think I should do? Kate . . . ?" Liz let out a long sigh. Seeing that her watch read ten o'clock, Liz yawned and stood up to leave.

That brought Kate back to reality. "Oh, honey, I'm sorry I'm not a very good listener tonight."

Liz took their glasses to the kitchen before heading toward the door. Kate helped Liz with her coat and scarf.

"I'm glad you asked me over, Kate. It gets pretty boring staying home each night with Mitch grading papers or talking on the phone with people in his department. This was fun," Liz said.

"No, Liz, I'm sorry for being such a bad friend tonight."

"Aw, forget it. You have plenty on your mind. Remember, you're coming over to our house for New Year's Eve. I'm making a seafood dinner and decorating with everything I collect at the beach."

"Liz everything you do is so creative. I still have the first assemblage piece you taught me to make in your art studio."

"Oh, you mean the cupid sitting on a swing inside a wire birdcage?"

"Yep. You're always trying something new in art. Now it's digital paintings of nature and jewelry made from beach glass or molds of small sea creatures."

"Well, I always knew I was no Da Vinci or Jackson Pollack, but I've always had an artistic urge inside me. Not having kids gave me lots of time to explore classes here and in the City. Thank God for Mitch. He's the calm, solid one. How he wound up with the Bohemian big mouth is still a mystery to me."

"Oh, I think he knows how lucky he is to have caught you. You're like an ocean of ideas with waves of creativity. And I'm so lucky you and I connected! I think back on those dull wine and cheese parties for visiting genius colleagues, those smug physics professors' wives. I wanted to scream each time Eric insisted I go with him to those boring evenings. Watching old *Friends* episodes on TV would have been more fun. But enough said about all that. I can't wait to try your luscious creations, so you know I'll be there." Kate kissed her friend goodbye, giving her a warm hug.

Liz opened the door, and feeling the blast of frigid air on her face, pulled her scarf tighter around the collar of her jacket.

Kate walked her friend down the steps and watched her get into her car, waving as Liz pulled away.

Still lost in her own musings, Kate slowly climbed the porch steps. The cold air lingered after she'd shut the door against the blustery snow, now falling inward. She felt sad again, and suddenly woozy. In her melancholy, or maybe because she felt the need to be punished, Kate sat on the kitchen barstool and dialed Eric's number.

In her sad, inebriated state, she hoped she might get some words of comfort from him. "I'm so lonely, Eric," she told him.

Instead, he replied, "Why don't you kill yourself then?" and hung up on her abruptly.

Kate walked upstairs to her bedroom and turned on the overhead lights. She reached into the dresser's top drawer, where she kept her tranquilizers. One by one, they fell from the bottle.

It took several minutes to wash them all down. Her throat felt scratchy from the pills. She woozily looked around. Her new tote bag was on the dresser. She reached into the black bag and took out a new lipstick. A surge of self-pity washed over her. *Who am*

I kidding? Lipstick is not going to do anything for me. I'm forty-three, but I feel sixty-three right now. She took the red lipstick and began to write on the bedroom mirror: *Why didn't any man ever love me?*

Kate sat on the floor. Her mind drifted . . . It didn't take long before she felt herself begin to lose her sense of control. Frantically, she picked up her phone and called her sister Rose, who lived an hour north. "I'm really scared," she said to Rose, and then started rambling.

"I'm coming down, honey. Let me call Mom and bring her with me on the drive. Stay calm. We're coming."

Kate tried to stay awake, tried to manage the thoughts swirling in her head. Looking out the window, she saw the soft snow falling even faster than earlier. Watching it come down very thickly was strangely tranquilizing.

I have to stay awake.

She looked in on the boys, still asleep in their bedrooms next to hers.

She went back to her room to lay down on her bed.

Nearly two hours passed before Rose and her mother ran into the bedroom at midnight, bringing a blast of cold air along with them.

"Why, Kate?" asked her anxious, somewhat angry-looking mother.

"I don't know. It just hit me that I was alone and no one cared about me. I called Eric. He told me to kill myself, so I thought, *Why not?* Then I felt scared and panicky.

From her bed, she heard her mother talking to the local cop in the doorway. He asked about the writing on the mirror, preparing to put it all down in his report.

She heard her mother pleading with the cop. "Officer," Alice said in her soothing, practiced voice, "Why put this in your report? What if the children wake up and see it, officer? Let's just erase what she wrote. She's been through hell these past months."

The cop thought a minute, and then Kate watched her mother erase the smeary words from the mirror. Kate could imagine her mother's inward relief and triumph.

"Divorce problems or not, we've got to take her to the hospital and get her stomach pumped out," the cop said. "Is there anyone who can watch the kids tonight?"

"Well," her mother answered, "maybe Kate's neighbors. They're pretty new to the neighborhood, but they seem to get along. You know, with the houses so far apart out here, it's hard to know anybody really well. But I think they would come over here."

"Call them right away, and let's get the kids taken care of for the night," he said.

Kate felt very woozy. Her eyelids heavy. She asked her mother to call Liz. "She should know, Mom."

Kate hazily felt herself put on a stretcher, noticing her odd clothing, a flannel nightgown with a puffy down jacket over top. Rose and her mother must have tried to get her out of the house before they called the police. She felt herself carried down the few front steps. The brisk air froze in her nostrils.

Kate woke up in the brightly lit hospital room. Standing next to her bed was Dr. Rossetti, the therapist she'd been seeing throughout the ordeal of her separation of six months.

Dr. Rossetti explained he'd sent her mother and sister home to rest and had assured the staff that last night's event was an aberration. The doctor looked at Kate, inviting her to talk.

"Dr. R. you know I'm not self-destructive. It's just been so hard going through this nightmare of a divorce. I took too many pills after having a few drinks . . . "

"I know, Kate. But if you want to keep your kids, this can't happen again. We need to talk about this. It's that serious. I know a great LCSW named Vinnie Green, who is a great, really involved, clinical counselor. He runs groups, mostly."

"Why a group?" Kate asked.

"To help you relate to others in a healthier way."

Dr. Rossetti's reply startled Kate. She was quiet for a moment. "Oh, I see . . . you've told me before that I spend too much time alone in my own head . . . "

Dr. Rossetti answered, "I only do private therapy with clients. Hearing from others will help you see you're not alone." He handed her a business card. "I'll let him know to expect your call."

"Okay, I'll call this Vinnie Green and make an appointment to meet with him first thing after the Thanksgiving weekend."

Dr. Rossetti spoke reassuring words, patted her hand, left the room.

After he departed, Liz returned to the room, got Kate ready to leave the hospital.

Kate replayed what had gone through her dazed mind while she was lying on the hospital gurney. She remembered a nurse asking her what had happened.

"Why did you take all those pills, honey?"

Slurring her words, Kate had sheepishly replied that her ex-husband had told her to do it. "I know he wants the kids."

"The bastard," said the nurse. "But don't worry now. We're going to get all that junk out of you, and you'll be yourself again."

Alice had been waiting for Liz's car to arrive, watching for her daughter's return from the large front windows of Kate's living room. Liz walked up the steps with Kate, the two women quietly talking. Alice opened Kate's massive red front door, thanked Liz for all of her help, and guided Kate toward the living room.

Kate said, "I feel so tired—tired, sad, and ashamed, Mom."

Kate stood still. There in front of her was Eric, pacing the rug, glaring at her, his face red with controlled fury. "How could you do this? Leave my children alone with strangers? I'm going to fight you for custody of them."

Kate couldn't speak. "Eric? What are you doing here?"

"Sorry, Kate," the soft female voice said. It was her neighbor Maddie. "When you went to the hospital, I stayed over with the boys. Harris called Eric, thinking he'd feel compassionate since he's the boys' dad. Eric came over this morning, then your family came back from the hospital, but I didn't want to leave until I knew you were all right. I hope you are." Kate didn't answer, and Maddie continued, "Harris and I were glad to look after the boys, and gladder now you're home."

Maddie's husband had called the one person Kate would never

have wanted to see, told him about her reckless act. So much ran through Kate's mind.

Maddie spoke up, "I can see you're okay, Kate, so I should go now. Your boys are playing in the backyard, making snow angels. They're good. They've eaten a good breakfast and don't know much of anything that's going on."

"Yes, my mom and sister can take things from here. I'll be fine. Thanks, Maddie, for everything."

"I'll show Maddie out," Alice said. "You go upstairs and lie down, Kate. Rose is up there straightening up your room."

"Eric's got the boys for Thanksgiving. I've got to sort that out."

"I'll speak to Eric and get him out of here, too."

Kate walked up the staircase. A shower, her bed, that's all she wanted.

Chapter

Two

Rose sat on the edge of the bed near Kate, listening to their mother's attempts to understand.

"Why did you write those words on the mirror?" Alice said testily. "Daddy loves you, even if he doesn't say it. And so what if Eric doesn't? He's crazy, anyhow. After he told you he'd been having an affair with the department secretary last year, you should have thrown the bastard out. But no, you had to save this marriage, for the children."

Kate sighed, feeling defeated, tired. "I don't know, Mom. I guess it was the drinks and the Ativan, plus feeling blue. I wasn't thinking. I just wanted it all to go away. I'm so weary. I need a break." She paused, and then added, "I want to rest here at home for a few days over the holiday. Skip Thanksgiving."

Her mother laughed, then spoke sternly. "Oh no, you *are* going to come to your sister's house for Thanksgiving. We're going to get on with life like none of this happened. Do you understand?"

"But, Mom, I don't have the strength to drive for hours in

holiday traffic, and then to face the family."

"You *will* come. Is that clear?" Her mother said it with great firmness. "You owe it to us after Rose and I drove down to deal with all of this."

"Mom, I'm fine, really. I just want some time to myself. I won't do anything stupid."

"Mom, listen to what Kate's saying. She doesn't need us disturbing her right now. She needs to sleep, and she needs her space," Rose said.

Kate's mom hesitated, then agreed. "Okay, I'll go back with Rose today then, but I don't want you here alone for too long. Promise you'll pack a suitcase first thing in the morning. You'll drive up early tomorrow, right?"

Kate felt mounting resignation. Her shame and sense of obligation let her know what was in store for her. No use fighting.

"What about the boys? And what about Winnie?" Kate said.

Alice spoke firmly, "We've told them you were a little under the weather, but that everything is fine and you just need a little break. Eric has agreed not to say anything to them about what happened. I'll help the boys get their things together and send them in to say goodbye before they leave. And Liz has already offered to take the dog for the weekend. Rose can drop her off. No more excuses, Kate. It's settled."

Chapter

Three

The next morning, Kate's long brown hair blew in the cold wind as she threw her suitcase in the trunk of her Explorer for the trip to Rose's house for Thanksgiving.

I can't believe I'm actually doing this, she thought, as her mother's edict replayed itself in her head. She put the car in gear and headed to the Chevron station to fill up with gas for the drive to Rockland County.

The sky was filled with clouds and hinted of more snow to come. The pre-Thanksgiving traffic was underway, and even the alternate local route was clogged. The only thing missing was the sappy holiday music on the radio. She put on an audio book, the latest Lee Child thriller, something to occupy her mind on the long trip to Rose's.

Kate had hours to think about her troubled life as she headed out in bumper-to-bumper highway traffic. *Eric. Eric. Eric. Why?* Her handsome, brilliant, take-charge husband, with his sarcastic wit and easy charm, had once worshiped her for her beauty and grace.

She recalled their first date. Their mothers had been friends at the Westchester country club both belonged to—at least Eric's mom had belonged to it before her acrimonious divorce. The two women played in the same weekly bridge game in Rye. Eric's Mom introduced them during his summer break from his PhD program at Stanford University, three thousand miles away. He was twenty-four, with the greatest smile and the deepest wide-set brown eyes she had ever seen. For Kate, it was love at first sight. Eric looked manly, unlike the college boys she usually dated. Kate had just finished her first year at NYU and was a total Anglophile. English literature was her first love—until Eric stopped talking with Alice and turned his gaze to her.

He became her first lover on their second date. For six weeks, their lust for each other was endless. Eric had an inventive energy. They went to horse races, placing meager two-dollar bets on long shots. Rode in the tunnel of love at amusement parks, kissing in the darkness. Attended esoteric plays Kate hardly understood, holding hands throughout.

When the time came for him to return to Stanford, Kate put on a happy face for him. They hungrily kissed as they had their time together as lovers.

Months went by too slowly for Kate. She kept at her studies in a distracted way, but her intelligence would not let her fail. Her brain was on autopilot.

Eric and she wrote back and forth, and her phone grew hot from their long-distance feverish chats. Christmas vacation finally came, and Eric flew back East. She went to JFK Airport with his mom and sister to meet his plane, scanning her eyes until she saw his long frame and big smile coming toward her. One month later, Eric impulsively asked Kate to marry him. It meant a move away from her close family, into the unknown of Northern California, but she quickly said yes. Three days later, they were in the sky heading for Palo Alto and a life together of bliss . . .

Eric was the answer for Kate's restless spirit. She had loved him crazily from day one. Even now, wishing him dead, she wanted the big life she'd had, the hungry sex. She missed the fighting and makeup sex. She wanted him back. *Sick . . . I have to stop this wildness and think rationally.*

Everything Kate had wanted, Eric laughed at, out of his jealousy and need to always be number one, in control. After his rant the day she kicked him out, Kate had managed to shout back at him, "I want my dream now! I want to finally use my brain! Wasn't I the one on the Dean's list for four years? Grad school was a breeze for me. Well, Eric, you know as well as I do that I'm very employable.

"Do you think anyone would hire you, a graduate of a university of rich but hardly genius-IQ students? And hardly any experience," Eric said, laughing. "I'll stop you any way I can. I'm the one with the clout, baby. The one who built a real career and got tenure. You didn't seem to mind being Mrs. Professor, as I recall! You loved me winning physics prizes, getting to spend a year at Harvard, a year at Princeton, even abroad in London for a year. You were so besotted with William Shakespeare and everything in England, you didn't even want to return home to the States."

"Your crazy genius has been more than enough for me," Kate retorted. Her face felt hot, but she yelled at him. "I had the kids and stayed home raising them because that's the way *you* wanted it. When did I have a chance to build a career? I did everything to help yours, and to raise our children. You asshole—you couldn't even balance a checkbook when I threw your sorry ass out. No wonder you wanted me at home. You were free to do whatever you wanted, knowing I was here to uphold the illusion of you as a family man. That way you could still screw Cathy, the married, bimbo department secretary who looked up to you. The only reason you stopped screwing her was because she got cancer and her hair was starting to fall out! Unbelievable that you confessed it to me the night before you left on a two-week sailing trip with Rich and Tom. Just left it in my lap and sailed off. It washed over me like filthy wake behind Rich's sailboat. You disgust me.

"But I have one secret of my own. Remember when we first started out at Cornell . . . all those faculty parties the seemed to buzz with great conversation, laughs and the thrill of meeting other young faculty members?

"We were only married a couple of years and leery you were always at someone else's side, showing off your great wit and flirting with any pretty graduate student. I needed excitement and closeness with someone who thought of me as brainy and beautiful, which was how you used to think of me. We hardly knew each other when I said yes to your impulsive marriage proposal, left everybody important to me, and flew across the country to begin what I imagined would be a fun and stimulating new life.

"That notion turned out to be a big laugh at my expense. I was feeling hopeless. Then all that changed during one faculty party. I remember I was walking around, a gin and tonic in hand, when I saw him—tall, young, and handsome. He had the most glorious blue eyes and thatch of tawny hair. I walked right up to him. Turns out he was a visiting professor from England. We hit it off—laughing, flirting, and completely at ease with each other. I boldly suggested we take a tour of the host's new downstairs addition.

"Mark and I had an instant attraction. I was the bold one and propositioned him at a physics department party . . . I knew it would be a short affair. His fiancée back in England would be coming over to the States to marry him in three months' time. Our affair began right away, meeting in different parts of the faculty town, his apartment, his car, up in Syracuse. We were besotted with each other. Mark was, is, the sweetest guy I've ever known. We got together for a short while after he married. He was the gentlest, sweetest lover. I missed him terribly after he went back to England two years later with his wife. I used to lie on the grass in the warm summer sunshine outside the house you and I were renting in Ithaca and cry."

Kate's voice rose in anger. "You fuck! You don't deserve to know what loving afternoons or nights we spent in each other's arms. You were so involved with your own quest for professional glory, or cheating on me, that you never caught on . . . I'm so glad I got to be one up on you!"

For a moment, Eric was seemingly distracted, then his face turned flush with anger and his usual look of disdain.

But now her story was out, and she could ignore Eric's bilious tirade.

Kate realized her loathing thoughts had taken over again. Perhaps some radio would calm her racing mind for the last few miles of the journey.

Chapter

Four

It was mid-afternoon when Kate's car pulled up the long, elegant driveway. Rose—the older sister, the dependable one, the one successfully married for twenty years, the designated family role model. Kate's mother was always holding Rose up as the very paragon of homemaking perfection and common sense. Rose's husband, Don Stanton, an easy-going, funny guy, consistently provided Rose and his family with the best of everything money could buy.

They had live-in help, a huge custom-designed house with two staircases—one an elegant curved staircase in the foyer for making grand entrances; the other in the rear for use by the live-in nanny and housekeeper. Several times a year, Rose, Don, and their equally fortunate friends enjoyed the high life on oceangoing cruise ships where they wore expensive evening gowns and tuxes and sat at the captain's table. Rose was serene and confident, devoid of the turmoil of her sister's chaotic, messy home life.

Kate, who had always wanted more, would go nuts if she had

to live like Rose. The thought made Kate's guilty self uncomfortable. It was Thanksgiving, and Kate needed to relax her restless brain, to curb her urge for revenge.

Marvelous smells were coming out of Rose's kitchen from the chopping, baking, and roasting of the day—yielding promises of delicious, stress-free, former Thanksgivings. This, at least, enabled Kate's shoulders to release some of the built-up tension of the past few days and the interminable ride across highways and bridges that had her nearly in tears—mixed emotions of sadness, anger, and frustration—feeling a of lack of control over anything in her life.

Kate's parents were already at Rose's house. Her father, William, was seated in the living room, smoking his usual Marlboros and reading the *Wall Street Journal*. He looked up, smiling, as Kate came into the room.

Jane, Kate's youngest sister, hummed while she set the dinner table. Jane was divorced and living with their mother and father, along with her three-year-old daughter, Amber. Jane had always been the so-called problem child of the family. Her divorce of a year ago had been a blow of sorts to Kate's mother, but now Jane was getting remarried, so her mother could relax and focus on Kate as the new black sheep of the family.

Promptly at six o'clock that evening, Nora, Rose's longtime family housekeeper, brought in an array of fastidiously prepared and fabulous-looking Thanksgiving platters of traditional side dishes, followed by the grand entrance of a perfectly golden-roasted turkey. Soon, wine glasses were filled, and Kate's father toasted his eldest daughter for her elegant job of chef and hostess.

Kate boiled with anger. Through all of her life, she had never got a compliment from him for anything. *Rose is the greatest because she can make a turkey!* Tipsy at another holiday gathering, Kate once laughingly asked her father if he loved her. His response was what she had known since the day of her fifth birthday, "Always."

More wine was poured after the turkey and trimmings were passed around the table. Finally beginning to relax and release the underlying tension of the day, Kate ate a little, although she still felt the strain of the past few days and the stressful drive to her sister's house.

The dinner plates were soon cleared by Rose to make room for coffee and desserts. Alice stood up from the table, huffily, to make an announcement, "Rose," she said, "Kate will stay here for the rest of the Thanksgiving holiday. Daddy and I are going to the Carlyle for the weekend with the Steins and Carpenters. We have theater tickets. We haven't been to the City since Jane and Amber moved in with us, and Daddy hasn't had a day off since the Hunter–Reynolds acquisition negotiations began."

Suddenly, Rose's composure exploded in a torrent of angry words directed toward her mother. "I have a life of my own, you know, Mother. You just throw these things out at me, and I'm sick of it. No matter how much I do, it's never enough for you. Kate is *your* child, you know. Just how big do you think my shoulders are?" she asked, crying as she spoke the words.

A deadly silence followed Rose's outburst. No one spoke, but the shock of her words left no place for anyone to speak. Rose left the room, her anger lingering in the dining room as she went. Don followed his wife.

After a few minutes of uneasy silence, Alice went to the hall, where her handbag lay on the entryway table. "Jane, Amber, Bill, we're leaving now. Get your coats. Hurry up." There was no attempt to soothe Rose with consoling words.

Kate sat in her chair, stunned, staring out the bay window as her parents and sister got into their sleek black Jaguar sedan. Rose watched the red of the taillights flicker as her father slowly backed down the steep driveway. Then they were gone. Kate stood transfixed.

Sadness washed over her. She remembered her father being so different when she was a young child. Kate recalled her fifth birthday, in the country in upstate New York, the last Saturday in June, hot and clear. Her mother, aunts, and cousins were all there for the summer, each family staying in a separate cabin. The lake gleaming in the hot sunshine. Her mother rocking Kate's four-month old sister in her arms. Kate had been so excited. Her mother had bought her a wonderful pinafore, designed with plump, red cherries on it. Soon her father would be arriving for the weekend. She had been so happy thinking of his coming up to the country for the weekend.

His car had pulled up at last. The tall, robust, youthful father got out, kissed her mother and tossed Kate up in the air. She giggled and felt safe in his strong arms. Her father told her that weekend was for them all to have fun. A big table was spread out with presents and a huge birthday cake for Kate, along with pitchers of lemonade and chocolate milk. Her relatives were all around, laughing. They sang "Happy Birthday" as she blew out six candles, including the one to grow on.

Her father's gift was the simplest and best, a butterfly net. He and she ran through the field of wildflowers, racing around, managing to catch some beautiful monarch butterflies, then setting them free. There were cherry trees all around. Her father reached up and picked a handful. Some of the cherries were doublets, two attached on either side. He put them on Kate's ears like earrings.

"Ruby earrings for my princess."

They both laughed at the image. She was so happy. He was her king.

How had she later found him so timid in the face of her mother's overbearing dictums? Gradually, Kate lost respect for him. Then she met Eric, her new king, a take-charge person, full of confidence. She had mistaken arrogance for confidence, bravado masking his actual insecurities.

Kate's childhood was one of security and family ties. No so for Eric's. Eric was a child whose life from the age of ten was near-total stress. His father and mother had separated after his father confessed he had met another woman and planned to divorce. As Eric stood watching, his angry mother had cut up all of his father's clothes. His father left them that day. Eric felt helpless and retreated to his room.

To escape the family turmoil, Eric began endless reading, brooding alone in his room, despising his mother's presence, blaming her for the loss of his father. His father had a very successful law practice, and the family enjoyed the many perks that came along with it. Eric and his younger sister, Victoria, had gone to fine sleepaway camps in summer. They were members of an exclusive country club in Rye, New York. Their life in Westchester County offered the best of everything. Golf for dad, bridge for mom, swimming for the kids. Eric loved his days playing in the clear blue pool while a nanny sat by in attendance. That all ended, especially for Eric. At age ten, when his father left the family, he lost more than just a dad.

Eric had been his father's favorite child. Then, suddenly, Eric lost the connection he had with his father. Eric became bewildered, bereft, and bad-tempered. From then on, Eric saw his father only once a month. His dad remarried, moved upstate, had another daughter, and became a county judge. A new family, a new child became his father's favorite and the recipient of his money and attention.

Kate's reverie ended. She sat alone at the dining room table, mulling over her options. Whether to go to Rose, who was sitting with Don in the family room, or stay in the dining room until someone came along to clue her in on what to expect next. Nothing felt simple any more. The whole situation made Kate sick. She sat there, alone, as the antique hall clock chimed.

Nine o'clock. There might be less traffic at this later hour. Fuck it! I want to sleep in my own bed. I'm leaving, and the hell with them all.

Her niece, Erin, came into the dining room. "Bye, Aunt Kate. I'm going to sleep over at my friend's house so we can hit the mall for Black Friday deals really early."

Kate looked at the fun-loving, sixteen-year-old girl standing in front of her, a blue overstuffed backpack on one shoulder. Not the scholarly type, Erin was glad there were no "stupid papers" to write or other homework assignments over the holiday break. Last year, Kate had heard Erin and a friend talking and laughing behind the garage, only to discover they were smoking pot. Erin begged Kate to keep quiet. Kate did, figuring Erin had enough troubles without her parents on her back about that too.

Rose and Don's eldest, Susan, was away at her college

boyfriend's house in Vermont. She skipped out on Thanksgiving at home this year, avoiding the typical family dramas. The two boys were at a concert starring a rock group with some crazy name. A long time ago she'd have known.

"I hope you'll still be here when I get back tomorrow, Aunt Kate. Tonight was crazy. Oh, well, see ya." Then, Erin was out the door. Kate heard her car pull away.

Kate walked into the family room, where Rose was sitting alone on the floral down-cushioned sofa. Don was nowhere in sight, probably had gone upstairs to bed. Rose yawned, resting her head on the back of the sofa. This was the warmest room, and the most natural room in Rose's big house. Everything was cushioned and comfortable. Oversized down-filled sofa, overstuffed chairs, all covered in a dark paisley pattern that added a feeling of intimacy to the room.

As soon as Kate entered, Rose got up and went to the fireplace, warming her hands by what was left of the fire Don had lit earlier in the evening.

Kate spoke to Rose. "I'm sorry you had to be part of 'that.' I know just what you mean, Rose." Kate felt the tiredness in her body, sighed, and went on, "Rose, I apologize for everything. I can't seem to get anything right these days."

"No, don't, Kate. You're my baby sister." Rose laughed. "Well, my nearly baby sister. Can't forget Jane and her dramas! I get so tired of Mommy always directing everyone's lives."

"I'm sorry for all the trouble I've caused you—and Don, too. Some holiday for him, eh?"

"Oh, you know Don." Rose smiled. "He's already arranged for us to go to Scotto's for dinner tomorrow night. On to the next thing before this one is even cleared away. And we really do want you to stay with us for the weekend. It's just that at my own table, I'd have like to be the one to bring it up."

Kate said, "I could kill Mom sometimes. She's so unconscious of anybody's feelings or plans, only focused on her own."

Rose picked up the newspaper from the end table, sat down and began flipping through the TV section. She started to giggle. "Guess what's on. Have you ever seen *Wuthering Heights* with

Laurence Olivier and Merle Oberon? It's coming on at midnight. Let's be bad girls! We can go upstairs to the sitting room and stay up and watch it. We can be smarter than all the fools lining up in the freezing night waiting for after-Thanksgiving sales!"

"I love it!" answered Kate. "We have enough time to get the kitchen cleaned up, and a reward to make it worthwhile."

Rose got up from the couch, stretching, a smile on her face. The sisters walked into the kitchen to clean up, as they had done together on many other holidays. The kitchen after-dinner scene looked a mess. Rose's beautiful Royal Worcester china, Christophle silver, Waterford wine glasses lay on the kitchen counters, serving island, sink. The sisters looked at one another and knew they had to do the cleanup themselves since Nora was off for the Thanksgiving weekend.

Nearly two hours later, the kitchen was finally back to normal. They took off their aprons. "Oh, thank God that's done with. My aching back," Rose said. "How're you doing, Sis?"

Kate groaned. "This is the ugly part of family holiday fancy dinners. Next time, let's order the Thanksgiving menu from your club. Please! Now, let's go in your sitting room and relax. We've both earned some R and R."

She looked up at Rose's flushed face. "Rosie, you and I are definitely getting to look more alike as we get older, except you have three inches of height on me."

"Kate, I thank you for that compliment. But you've got the large green eyes I've always envied. Mine are a kind of blah hazel color."

"No putting yourself down for anything, Rose. Now, let's go watch *Wuthering Heights*. What a great choice—not the usual *Sound of Music* or *The Wizard of Oz* or Christmas movie!"

Once in the sitting room, Rose turned on the TV, and they sat down beside each other on the big, comfortable sofa. Rose fiddled with the remote while Kate laid an afghan over them both. The movie began. Kate and Rose lounged on the sofa, pretending to swoon over young Olivier's handsome, brooding Heathcliff until the credits ended.

They hugged goodnight, each going to her own bedroom, feeling like naughty, but happy, girls again.

Chapter

Five

F riday morning, Kate rose to see the sun glistening upon the thick layer of fluffy snow outside her window. Although it was nearly eleven o'clock, the house was quiet. Kate made herself a pot of coffee and walked down the driveway to get the *New York Times*. She looked at the paper as she walked the boundaries of the property, enjoying the crisp air. The newspaper was thin, most of its contents made up of early Christmas sale ads.

Kate looked in through the garage door. She overheard Don, sitting in his garage workshop, talking on his cell phone, finalizing plans to visit his parents for Christmas. Don spotted Kate, smiled, finished his phone call.

"Hi, Don," Kate said, walking into the garage.

"Hi, Kate. I'm just heading out to shovel the driveway. Did you sleep well?"

"I did! Rose and I stayed up watching *Wuthering Heights*, and I slept in till eleven."

"That's great. I hope you get a nice break being here, Kate. I know things have been rough for you."

"I like the peace and change of scenery up here, Don. Thank you for having me."

"Don't be silly, Kate. You know we love you. After all, we've known each other since you were eight. Since I threw you in the ocean to teach you how to swim!"

This was a standing joke with them. "Don, you are a great guy! I'm so glad you and Rose are part of my life. I envy Rose for having such a mellow guy like you for a husband. You complement each other."

True, they were both into the more material things of life—trips, furnishings, cars. Yet, they had kept the same group of friends for years and years. Don had added a little paunch to his middle but remained in pretty good shape. "How have you managed to look so good after all these years?"

"I'm a lucky guy. Maybe I'm not the six-foot-five, athletic guy a lot of gals as great as Rose would have chosen. I might be stout, but I'm strong and handsome," he said, brushing his hands through his dark brown hair, salted at the temples with gray. Don stood up, facing Kate with a grin on his face.

Laughing now, Kate said, "You're tall in everything that really counts in my eyes."

"That driveway's not going to take care of itself." Don put on his thick wool plaid jacket and heavy boots, preparing to go shovel. Don commanded Misty, their big sweet collie, and Charlie, their little black rescue pooch. In a flash, they were at his heels, ready to go outside with Don.

"I'm going to take a short walk around the neighborhood and leave you to get on with your chores," Kate said, and headed down the driveway.

Don and Rose had shared lives together. Their children, spaced three years apart, had grown up together. After Susan's birth, Rose remained at home. She became more involved in the community as each successive child came along. She was on the board of several charities in the township and was extremely organized and successful at fundraising. Kate looked to Rose as a model of calm and contentment.

The mainstay of Kate's friendships had always come from Eric's faculty mates. Kate's other friends were the mothers of her kids' friends. Beyond a little chit chat when dropping off or picking up the kids, the only time Kate spent with friends came at their weekly bridge game.

Plenty kept Kate busy: PTA fundraisers, Halloween gatherings, holiday concerts, to name but a few. Kate lived the life of a responsible mom, her only rebellion a few private cigarette breaks each day. Eric hated her smoking, and it drove her mother wild. Kate found the rituals of smoking a release. Those, plus the seemingly endless cups of coffee, kept her going each day. The approach of winter brought on feelings of gloom—the short days of limited sunlight, layers of heavy clothing, chilly air creeping in through the door gap . . . and the increasing demise of her marriage.

After her split from Eric, many of the faculty wives, the school moms, too, all drifted away, uncomfortable inviting a fifth-wheel to their dinner parties. Kate relied on Debbie Roberts, whose son Matt was a classmate of Ryan's. Debbie lived on her street, one of the few neighbors who was divorced herself. She helped Kate out with ferrying the boys around town. They sometimes met up during her walks with another near neighbor a couple of blocks over. Then there was Liz.

Liz didn't live close by, but she was close in heart. Liz had already invited Kate to her New Year's Eve party. Kate accepted right away, grateful to have something festive on the calendar. Liz helped Kate through what had been a rough year. She could confide in Liz.

Then, of course, the weekly therapy group would be starting soon. Oh, how she dreaded going to those meetings, overwhelmed by the thought of sharing her overdose, hospital story, messy life. The image of herself stumbling through an explanation made her wince. But group was more than a week away, by then she might have a better understanding and be able to share. In her heart, Kate knew true healing and understanding would take a much longer.

She envisioned Dr. Rossetti's handsome, concerned face and caring voice. Dr. Rossetti talked about realistic expectations. Kate had put the burden on Dr. Rossetti to explain—let the therapist figure out how to get her through this mess of emotions. Kate wanted to make sense of how the love that Eric and her had could turn to such hatred. The marriage was over, but the hurt was not.

At one time, her love for the brooding genius she knew Eric to be had trumped everything else in Kate's existence. She used to imagine that being married to Eric was what being married to Beethoven would have been like. Kate had once written that sentiment in a letter to her mother when on their first sabbatical year in London, before the kids arrived in their lives. From the start, the kids made the marriage worth all its struggles. Eric actually cried with joy when the gynecologist had called to say she was pregnant the first time.

So much had changed over the years. Now, with Eric's creative juices dried up, Kate became the someone to blame for his sense of failure. Kate had suggested this to the good doctor in one of their private sessions. Dr. Rossetti had answered her by nodding yes and explaining, "It's like chess players, Kate. They peak early. So do most mathematicians. I'm not sure if that's true of other disciplines like physics, though . . . but if we think about it rationally, there's likely something more going on."

Kate had wanted an exciting life, with a brilliant yet funny man, and she wanted to travel, to enjoy the prestige of being the wife of someone who would take her away from the New York area and her often judgmental mother. And she wanted that education of her own so badly. She'd always had a quick, literary mind. *Where was that mind these days?*

Kate had circled the block, coming back to stand in front of Rose's house. She snapped back to reality, realizing she had been zoning out. The emotional fatigue of the past few days lingered.

Kate walked into a kitchen filled with the aroma of coffee. Rose stood in a lounge suit and apron, cradling a coffee cup. Smiling at Kate, Rose put her cup down on the counter and pulled a pretty floral mug from the cupboard.

"I know you've always liked this cup."

Rose, ever the hospitable hostess, poured and handed Kate her cup of coffee and motioned for her to sit down at the checkered-cushioned breakfast nook.

Even Rose's kitchen was a dream fulfilled. Rose had remodeled with all sorts of cabinetry and built-ins. One cabinet opposite the refrigerator held a mini dessert station, with huge canisters of pourable chocolate syrup, chopped nuts, colored sprinkles, and more. It was like Willie Wonka's factory, containing all the forbidden treats of childhood. At their own childhood home, their after-school snack consisted of a plastic-wrapped Hostess cupcake and a glass of white milk. After dinner, a piece of fruit constituted dessert. So, this indulgence was Rose's rebellion. Kate loved it!

Rose offered Kate an English muffin, and then split and put them in the toaster oven.

"Have you talked to your boys?"

"I miss them so much when they're away, but it's impossible to call them while they're at Eric's house."

"That's fine, honey. They know you love them," replied Rose, carrying a tray that had a fancy butter dish, a honey pot, and several jars of jam.

"Don made a seven o'clock reservation at Scotto's Restaurant for us. Is there anything you'd like to do today, or someplace you'd like to go this afternoon? I know you hate the idea of all the crowds at the mall, but I know some really nice boutiques. We could go out and browse . . . or maybe you just want to stay in and relax. Think about it, and we can decide later."

"If you don't mind, Rose, I think I'd prefer just staying in, maybe reading the book I brought along and taking a nap before we head out to Scotto's. I'm sorry I'm not much fun. Do you think you'll go out shopping anyway?"

"I have piles of clothes to go through. I'm going to organize my clothes closet and Don's too. With winter seriously here now, I need to sort through my seasonal clothes. I think this November is the latest Thanksgiving has been in years."

Kate looked out the kitchen window. The panes had frosted over. The snow had started falling again, and she could see the neighbors' children, home for Thanksgiving, sledding down their own long driveway.

Don came back inside, dogs at his heels, and shook the snow off his boots. He hung his jacket up on a hook in the mudroom.

"Ooh, it's cold out there. Any coffee left?" His cheeks were bright red. Seeing Rose already taking a mug from the cupboard, he sighed and sat down to wait for his coffee.

Rose poured Don a cup of the remaining coffee and talked to him about what he'd like to eat after his exertions outdoors.

Kate said, "I'll leave you two alone. I'm going to do some reading and take a hot bath, if you don't mind."

"Oh, please, go right ahead. There's some wonderful bath oil in the guest bath. I picked it up the other day from this great new boutique."

"I noticed you put some great smelling stuff out for me, Rose. Thanks, babe. See you both later." Kate needed some time to relax and think.

Kate straightened her bed and lounged on top of the ivory coverlet, pulling a cozy hand-knitted blanket over herself and settling in with her journal and favorite pen. After writing down her thoughts, Kate drew herself a bath, took in the aroma of the various bath products, and settled on lavender-scented bubbles. The luxurious bath relaxed Kate, so much so that she soon fell asleep in the tub.

Arousing herself, she glanced up at the small window in the bathroom and noticed how dark the day had become.

It was time to start getting ready for dinner with Rose and Don. The restaurant, after all, was thirty minutes away. It would be packed, likely they'd wait for a table even with reservations.

Kate picked out the only dress she had brought along from her home. The striped, jersey dress looked fine on her, despite the weight she had recently lost.

Kate could hear Don and Rose laughing downstairs at something. With her Armani makeup done nicely, diamond stud earrings sparkling, and mile-high, black expensive designer heels on, Kate walked slowly downstairs. Rose and Don were also ready for their night out. "You both look great. I'm a lucky guy tonight!"

In the car, Kate listened to the local station Don had on the radio.

"Can you believe they're already playing Christmas carols?" he said. "I'll never get used to starting Christmas so early. Why I should be surprised by now, I don't know."

Don was a smooth driver, and they arrived at Scotto's in good time. She inhaled the delicious, garlic-scented food being brought out on trays as they waited for their reserved table. "I love Scotto's. It's such a great idea to have delicious Italian food instead of Thanksgiving leftovers."

The large dining room was warmed by a huge central wood-burning fire, glowing and crackling away in the fireplace. Before too long the three of them were sliding into their red leather booth. Don and Rose sat next to one another with Kate sitting facing them. The waitress took their order for drinks.

Kate ordered hers first. "It's a Scotto's special holiday margarita for me. Make it a large one."

Kate sipped her margarita, savoring the salt around the rim of the glass. "I already feel relaxed. The ambiance of this restaurant is always amazing." They talked and drank until their server came to the table to take their meal order.

"I'll have the house Caesar salad. Then your fabulous linguine with white clam sauce. Yum!" Kate said.

Rose ordered Chicken Piccata with a side order of zucchini and marinated artichokes.

Don said, "I'd like the broiled branzino fish and a side of spaghetti with marinara sauce." The waitress took their menus.

She returned with a covered basket of hot, crusty Italian garlic-herb rolls. What a happy alternative to Thanksgiving leftovers! Don ordered a second round of drinks, his arm around Rose's shoulders.

"This is great. Two very dirty martinis and two gorgeous gals. Am I a lucky bastard tonight or what?" Don looked directly at Kate. She smiled back at him. Suddenly, Don blurted out, "Why did you do it, Kate? You're a young, beautiful woman, with everything to live for—two great kids, a family who adores you . . . What's gotten into you? You've always seemed so pulled together, so normal."

Kate felt her heart beating very fast, a mixture of shock, anger, and sadness. What nerve he had. What gave him the right to confront her, or rather ambush her, as if he was so certain, so right, to make a judgment, and one that was so wrong? No words came to her. She was aware of how trapped she felt. Tears of anger filled her eyes, but she was determined they should not fall.

Kate gulped down the rest of her drink, deciding not to answer Don at all. If she could just get through the meal, in an hour or so she could be back at the house. Kate decided that in the morning she would quickly repack her suitcase and drive home.

But the tears began to fall, despite her intention to be in control.

"Honestly, Kate, I never felt Eric deserved you, and I've known you since you were a child. You're a talented, beautiful young woman who deserves more, and I promise you that two years from now, you will find a man who will love you the way I love your sister."

Rose smiled, basking in the love she felt coming from her husband. Kate sat there, feeling like a tiny, helpless child being thrown again into a cold ocean against her will, without her permission, all for a good cause: to teach her to swim.

Somehow, they managed to get through dinner. They passed on dessert, but Don downed a glass of port before calling for the check.

They stood to leave. "I can help myself with my own coat, Don." Kate felt her cheeks burning with unexpressed anger.

The three got into Don's Jaguar and started the journey back to their house in silence. Sitting in the leather back seat, Kate fidgeted.

"Looks like an accident on the highway ahead," Don said. "Probably someone had too much post-Thanksgiving booze."

"I wish I'd had a third margarita myself," Kate mumbled. Kate was shocked by the resentment she felt rising for the brother-in-law she always had loved and admired. She knew Don meant well, but he had disregarded the circumstances that had driven her to the action of the other night. Yes, she would escape all this, but who knew what "normal" meant anymore. Holidays with Eric and the boys, that was normal. Again, she felt the crazy need to hear Eric's voice. She needed to see her boys. She was all neediness.

The three of them walked into the house in silence. Kate felt compelled to call Eric and tell him she was coming home and had to see the children. She figured his latest girlfriend would be tired by now of spending her Thanksgiving days off from work watching her boyfriend's kids.

"I have them until six o'clock Sunday," Eric said. "That's when you'll get to see them." With a sneer in his voice, he added. "Happy Thanksgiving, bitch."

Chapter

Six

Rose was upset when Kate told her the next day that she was feeling fatigued and would be driving home early. Eric had the kids until Sunday, but at least she'd have time to get the house cleaned, bake some cookies, buy groceries. Kate didn't dare be late receiving the kids from Eric. God forbid she got delayed at the store and was not back by six o'clock on the dot.

Kate was too ashamed to tell her sister that on a previous occasion when she was late, Eric had threatened to leave the kids at a police station somewhere, and she would have to figure out which one it was.

Kate wearily packed, thanked her sister for everything, and got in her car, eager to get home before the autumn darkness set in.

"Call me when you get in," said Rose. "I want to know you got home safely."

Kate reassured her she would do just that.

"And no more funny stuff, okay?"

Kate merely sighed and nodded.

At least the reverse trip was not as anxiety provoking as the ride to Rose's house had been. She put the car into the garage and went inside. Hungry, but she pushed herself to put away the contents of her suitcase before going into the kitchen.

Rose had packed up some Thanksgiving leftovers and the remains of her unfinished meal from Scotto's. The Caesar salad was soggy, so she discarded that and settled on reheating some of the juicy littleneck clams and linguine in a small pot on the Viking kitchen range top.

While she prepared her food, Saturday night filled her mind. How should she pass the rest of the evening until she felt tired enough to sleep through the night and could wake enthusiastic about Ryan and Josh's return?

Kate felt too restless to read and too sad to do anything much else. She took her plate to the living room and turned on a mindless TV show.

Before long, she had finished her meal and regained some of her energy. In the kitchen, she cleared out the old food from the refrigerator, washed up the dishes, wiped down the fridge shelves and kitchen counters.

Feeling satisfied to have restored order to the kitchen, Kate went upstairs to turn on the shower in her tiled bathroom. The hot shower relaxed her, and when she came out she picked up the Saturday morning paper and sat down in her reading chair. Kate liked to do the daily *New York Times* crossword puzzle, and looked forward most of all to the Sunday puzzle. She was proud that she always did them in ink, nearly always finishing them. Before long, drowsiness overtook her. After a last smoke, she called it a night.

Kate awoke to bright sunlight. For a moment, she forgot she was home. Kate, sighed and felt relieved at the thought of not having to deal with anyone again today—except for her darling eleven-year-old Ryan and eight-year-old Josh who'd be coming home later that day from Eric's.

Her psyche was bruised, and she felt angry with herself for being a coward in not telling Don or her mother to stay out of her life. Lately, everything felt like a trap. When she had gone to the gynecologist a couple of weeks earlier for a checkup, Kate even had to listen to his recriminations. He explained away her abdominal pains, implying they were psychosomatic. Kate questioned whether her miscarriage two years ago might be the cause. Dr. Rossetti had even suggested she harbored resentment about having children.

Kate got out of bed and went to the door for her *Sunday Times,* happy to sit with the crossword and start the day slowly. She made coffee and sat in her silky midi length floral Natori robe and matching nightgown with thin straps, gulping down her first cup of strong black Italian roast coffee along with a piece of buttered toast.

She felt logy today, the stress of the past few days making her head throb. She startled at the sound of the kitchen phone's jarring ring. "Oh, my head."

Kate said a weak hello into the mouthpiece of the phone. Rose's voice sounded annoyed to her still slightly hungover condition. "You were supposed to call me and let me know you had got home safely, remember?"

Kate let out a long sigh. With irritation rising in her throat, she found the will to let Rose know she was fine. "Were you worried I'd killed myself? I *do* feel semi-dead today, I'll admit, after Friday night's attack from Don."

"Not funny, Kate," was Rose's reply. "How are you going to spend the day, Kate?"

"Please, Rose, get off my back. You're beginning to sound like Mom. I'm perfectly capable of being by myself without something dire happening."

In the moments of silence that followed, Kate could sense Rose searching her mind for the right reply.

"Thanks for caring so much about me, Rose. I love you so much. I'm fine. I really am. I'll call you later this week. Promise."

"Fine," Rose said, and the phone call was over.

Kate spent the day keeping busy—tidying house, straightening the boys' closets, doing some restocking at the Grand Union Supermarket, and baking the boys' favorite: chocolate chip pecan cookies. To most, it would seem like mindless activities, but it was like therapy after the abortive time at Thanksgiving. By the time she was done, she had no energy left to cook a meal. *Oh, well, I guess Heather and Eric fed them something today. Probably Frosted Flakes for breakfast and Jack in the Box for lunch. If old Mom has to give them some canned soup and tuna sandwiches for supper, so be it.*

A little past six-thirty, Heather drove up with the boys. The eighteen-year-old Britney Spears petite blonde was Eric's latest conquest. She looked like a waif. Yet, Kate was happy to see her—at least she would be spared Eric's sarcasm. Not forever, she knew, but at least for today. After a few polite words to one another, Heather drove away in her dented Honda Civic. Kate walked into the house with the boys. That took care of that.

Hugging Ryan and Josh to her, Kate felt her heart expand with the love she felt for them. To them, she wasn't a loser, a bitch, or a pitiful girl who had failed at so much in so many peoples' eyes. To them, she was Mom, and that was enough for her. Being a good mother was the one role everyone agreed she did well.

"How was Thanksgiving?" she asked them.

Ryan said they'd had a lot of pizza and takeout and watched the Macy's Parade on Daddy's TV with Heather.

"So it was fun, though Daddy slept a lot because he said he'd got a cold from some of his dumb students. Yesterday, he bought us a bunch of stuff, but we have to keep them at his house. We can play with them when he gets us next weekend," said Josh. Josh was a chubby, lively boy. Not much bothered him. Kate smiled and hugged her younger son.

"You can tell me more about the stuff he bought you while we get you unpacked and ready for school tomorrow. I drive the carpool this week, so I need us all to be organized and out the door on time."

Josh asked about their terrier pup. "I missed having Winnie sleep with me on my bed."

"I know you did, sweetie. But now you're home, so tomorrow night she'll jump up onto your bed and keep you snuggly warm."

"I wish we could get her from Liz's tonight."

"Winnie will be here when you get home from school tomorrow,

I promise."

"It smells good in here, Mom," Ryan said. "Kinda like cookies or something."

"That's exactly what it smells like. I made chocolate chip cookies for you two. When you're finished unpacking, you can come back down and have some."

The boys talked about their game while they headed upstairs to unpack. Kate heated the soup, made sandwiches, poured milk, and set out the plate of cookies.

After they'd eaten, Kate went upstairs to run the bath. She focused on the moment: the warm water running into the bathtub, the joyful sounds of the boys' happy chatter, the gratitude of having a family. While the boys bathed, Kate sorted the dirty clothes and started the wash.

She returned upstairs, catching sight of Ryan in the bathroom brushing his teeth. "Just look at you, Ryan. You look like you grew two inches since last weekend. Impossible that my eleven-year-old handsome boy is a tween. Well, at least you're not too old to give your mom a kiss goodnight."

After months of this life, traveling between her house and Eric's, the two young boys no longer asked why their parents didn't spend holidays or birthdays together with them. The overwhelming sadness took hold of Kate again. She took deep breaths to stop the panic rising in her chest as she imagined how their first split Christmas would be. Everything felt out of her control—so much to adjust to and plan for, with the boys growing so quickly—and she had no energy or resolve to move forward. No solutions were forthcoming. Not tonight.

Chapter

Seven

Monday morning came quickly. Kate had the boys in the SUV and was dutifully making the stops to pick up the boys' schoolmates in the carpool. Bellville Street Elementary started at eight o'clock. Then Kate had stops to the cleaners, gas station, and library, then finally on to Liz's to pick up Winnie.

Around nine-thirty, Kate parked her car in the garage and walked into the house, bringing Winnie with her. Her phone rang just as she plugged it in to recharge. Leaning over the kitchen counter, staring at the name on the screen, Kate took a deep breath before answering.

Her neighbor skipped the niceties and started straight into her reason for calling, "Hi Kate. It's Maddie. You looked so pale when I saw you driving the boys to school. I want you to know that I'm here for you if you need anything, anything at all. How about we get together? You know you can always talk to me."

Kate couldn't hide the irritation she was feeling at that moment.

She snapped at Maddie. "I wish everyone would stay out of my life for a change. What happened, happened, and I'm sick of having everyone dissect my every movement."

"No need to bite my head off, Kate, I just thought we could go for a walk, that would be nice to do together. There are things I wanted to share with you."

"Maddie, don't you ever get tired of being a do-gooder?" Kate reached for the pack of Virginia Slims on the counter and lit one, inhaling as deeply as she could, flicking the ashes into the sink.

"I don't think you're being fair, Kate. I'm just concerned about you. You did go to the hospital in the middle of the night to get your stomach pumped out—"

"And how many people have you told about that, Maddie?"

"It's no secret, Kate. Things like that don't happen in this town without people blabbing about it with each other. And as for my life being so perfect, I could tell you things that would shock you to your shoes."

Now Kate's interest was aroused. She stubbed out her cigarette and threw it into the sink, letting cold water drip on it. "What are you talking about, Maddie?"

"Let's get out for a walk and maybe I'll tell you about it. Maybe then you can focus on someone else instead of just feeling the world is out to get you. You don't hear yourself and how much you're caught up in your own problems."

Kate felt herself calm down a notch. "If you promise not to preach to me, I guess we can get out and walk, but just for a bit. I'm tired and cranky from the shitty Thanksgiving I had, so don't expect any long heart-to-hearts from me.

"Believe me, Kate, you just aren't that fascinating to me at the moment. And if you don't want to go at all, that's just fine with me. I'm only suggesting a walk. You don't have to bite my head off. If you don't want to see me, say you don't want to. And when you've had enough, you can leave."

With that agreement, they met for a walk. Kate and Maddie walked on the trail, the autumn leaves crunching under their boots and the scent of a wood fire on the air. Kate, though still wary, began to relax as they walked through the woods surrounding their neighborhood. Kate's mind was wandering. Still feeling uncomfortable, she tried to be civil.

Hesitantly, Maddie started to speak. "About four years ago, Harris came home from his practice and told me he didn't love me anymore. He just bluntly came out and said he wanted a divorce. I was beyond crushed. I couldn't believe what he was telling me. There was no other woman involved, and it wasn't anything I had or hadn't done. He said he wanted a divorce, and his mind was thoroughly set on it. I couldn't wrap my head around it. Everything went blank. All I kept thinking was that I wanted to die. That night he packed up a suitcase and told me he was going to a hotel. Before I knew it, Harris was gone from the house, and I was left alone. I was in total shock and denial. I didn't think I could live without him. I didn't want to. It all seemed like a nightmare. That night I went into the bathroom, took a razor blade, and slit both of my wrists."

Kate stopped walking. "What am I hearing here, Maddie?" Kate stared into Maddie's eyes, disbelieving, and her mind raced on.

"That's not the end of the story," Maddie said. "I'll tell you the rest, if you're ready to hear it."

Kate nodded, and Maddie went on. "Harris happened to have forgotten some of his medical supplies and returned home to get them. He found me bleeding and unconscious on the floor of the bathroom that adjoins his home office. He called 911. I was rushed to St. Joseph's. Then, when he was told I was out of danger, he left again.

"My near death didn't send him rushing back into my life with remorse in his heart. He still wanted to divorce me. My parents tried to help me cope, but I was numb in my body and dead in my spirit. After I was released from the hospital and had time to think, I told my lawyer I wouldn't stand in Harris's way regarding the divorce, but that I needed a year before I'd sign the papers. I needed time—for my sanity, for acceptance, and for setting out a new path. I didn't want alimony or support of any kind, just time. Harris agreed to delay the final divorce papers for one year. I took off for Canada and lived in a retreat house."

Kate's voice was quavering as she began talking, "You went to Canada and stayed for a year?"

"Nearly a year. On the day before our divorce was to become final, I got a call from Harris. He told me he loved me and wanted us to stay together. I've never told anyone else this, Kate, though I'm sure there've been plenty of rumors about it. I haven't offered anyone any explanations. I've kept it to myself, the same as you are doing now. But after all you've been through, I want you to have hope. I nearly died, nearly ended my life. Now I have life growing in me, and my marriage is stronger than ever. God does work miracles."

Kate couldn't take the sanctimonious chatter any longer. She stopped walking and began to shout. "Maddie, Eric is not Harris! He's not coming home, and frankly, I don't think I want him back. But thanks for the walk."

Kate hiked off and was soon back in her own house. She lay down on the sofa, no energy even to take off her down parka. She didn't give a damn.

Kate woke up to the sound of her own snoring. Maddie's revelation had both shocked her and made her feel even sadder. She looked at the time on her phone. Ten to three! The kids! She had to pick up the kids! Kate threw on her red wool coat, grabbed her car keys, and headed out to her SUV to pick up the boys.

Chapter

Eight

Wednesday morning, Kate put a call into Dr. Rossetti's office, hoping to get the answering machine, hoping he'd release her from the upcoming meeting he'd set up with Vincent Green, take care of the cancellation. No luck. Dr. Rossetti reinforced his endorsement of Vinny and group therapy. He reassured her, "You can do this, Kate. Just go."

"Call me Vinny. We're all on first names in group. If you feel comfortable sharing, then share. At the start, just say your name and why you're joining the group. No pressure," Vinnie had said. But he said it with expectation that Kate would share more than she was anticipating right there in his office.

Vinny looked a far cry from Dr. Rossetti, who always wore a dress shirt and sport jacket, matching his clothes to the formal approach of his therapeutic style. Vinny 's eyes were encircled by John Lennon type wire-framed glasses. His outfit, a plaid flannel shirt, jeans with rolled bottoms, and worn tan suede cowboy boots. His large feet were propped up on a swivel chair. As he rocked back and forth, he leaned forward to focus on Kate. She wriggled around a bit, her hands crossed over her chest. Uneasy.

"This group thing may be a little too laid-back and touchy-feely for me. I'm not sure it's my thing."

"You'll have to come next week and find out, won't you?"

This was the week. This Thursday, she would have to force herself to go to the meeting and tell the group everything.

The week dragged by, day by endless day. Kate felt sad, then numb, finished but not dead.

Finally, the day came when she was scheduled to confess her actions of the past Thanksgiving to her new weekly therapy group. Women's Lib had never done much for Kate over the years, except to make her feel inadequate for being "just a mom." She had been to encounter groups off and on, for what seemed like forever, listening to all the B.S.

She remembered one session when she got up her courage to tell the story of her childhood, to reveal some of her pain. She had been shot down by one woman who said, 'Frankly, we've all been where you are now, and we're through with that subject now."

Well, so much for the Gloria Steinem sisterhood. Kate never went back to the group. Lately, a vodka and tonic and some Katy Perry CDs were sufficient to mask the problem.

After she and Eric separated, Kate had begun seeing Dr. Rossetti, on Liz's recommendation. Feeling guilty about her lack of maternal feelings had sent Liz to Dr. Rossetti. Eric and Kate had set their academic ambitions and private freedom above everything else.

It had seemed strangely dangerous when Dr. Rossetti calmly and privately advised Kate as to what she really needed, which was to be in a group where she would get useful feedback. Kate fought her skepticism, but agreed to try it out, at least for a while.

Kate delivered her instructions to Robin, the kids' regular teen-age babysitter, and reinforced her expectations to the boys before getting in the car and heading to group therapy. As she drove, she tried to rehearse what she would say in group.

Promptly at seven, Vinnie laid the groundwork for Kate's story. The atmosphere was relaxed, casual. Everyone was either sprawled out on the benches or sitting in the comfortable chairs that swung around, back, and forth. After Vinnie prepared them for Kate's share with the group, he directed everyone's attention to Kate.

Kate began to speak. Her mixture of shame and nervousness brought the pain to the surface, and her story came rushing out in a torrent. "Right before our Thanksgiving break, I took an overdose of pills with some alcohol. I thought at the time it was just something silly, something to give me a little peace from my ex. Eric is constantly harassing me. Stupid me called him, thinking I just wanted some kind words from his mouth to my ears. He used to be able to make me feel better with a few choice words of reassurance. I expected to hear that he was sorry about our divorce.

"Really, I know better. Of course, he said something cruel. This is the new Eric, and the reality of our current relationship. He told me to kill myself. Then he hung up on me. So, I took more pills and swallowed them down with a glass of gin. Afterwards, I called a friend, feeling high, but doing my best to sound happy, to join me for a drink or two." Kate hesitated, remembering the feeling of despair. She stifled the sobs rising in her throat.

Out of the group of eight, Patsy was the one who spoke, "What a fucking bastard that guy is. Someone ought to kill him!"

Vinnie gently laid his hand on Patsy's arm. "Patsy, save whatever you have to say until Kate finishes telling her story to the group."

Kate was starting to feel drained and wanted to stop hearing her voice repeating her shame. She looked down at her lap. "It's a long story, but the upshot is that my sister and mother drove down, the police came, and I had my stomach pumped out."

Vinny looked around at the group and said, "Let's go around the room and tell Kate how her story impacted us."

At that moment, Kate's eyes wandered up to the fading Abraham Maslow poster on the wall: "I'm all right; you're all right. We're not put here on earth to make each other happy. But if we meet, it's beautiful."

Kate hated it. She pointed to the quotation and said, "I wonder if that includes torturing somebody to the brink of suicide."

"Kate, a torturing person is a tortured person."

"A torturing person is a tortured person? I don't get it," Kate spat out.

The group fell quiet, then Rhoda said, "I feel so hurt for your pain, Kate. Don't be ashamed. We've all been in bad places and didn't know how to make the pain go away."

Kate let her tensely folded arms speak for her. Vinnie's idea of group help was getting trite by now. She sat still, her body rigid and her eyes fixated on the poster on the wall, feeling like a fucking victim being judged by a room full of trauma victims even worse off than herself.

Normally shy, Eden spoke out suddenly, "Vinnie, I know it's usually against your rules for the group, but couldn't Kate call one of us if she's feeling desperate? What if it helps her to reach out? Please, Kate, you don't have to feel alone anymore."

Vinny shook his head, tapping his sheaf of notes. "Calling is a no-no. Kate has to bring her thoughts and feelings to group."

Kate answered, fuming, "That's the stupidest advice I have ever heard. What is that, therapy cop-out talk? I know why they call therapy 'psychobabble.'"

She grabbed her things and ran out of the session room.

As she approached her car, Kate heard someone calling her name. Jessica had followed her to her car. "Kate, what you need is to get out of the house and start dating again. You know my husband, Steve, is a lawyer, and he can get you a date any time. You're a beautiful, vibrant woman, and you deserve to be free of this shithead already. Don't call your husband. Don't talk to him, and don't let him bring you down. My life didn't end when I was raped, and yours doesn't have to end either. You do know this crap Eric does to you is a kind of rape, right?"

Kate snapped at Jessica, "You think a date is what I need? You know what I really need, Jessica? I need a life of my own. Eric gets me so angry and confused that I forget it's my time. I always wanted to be an English professor, one who really helps young people to learn. Alright, I didn't go to Harvard or Yale, but I could hold my head up because my head was where my heart was. Eric laughed at me. Said I wasted all my university years on nothing worthwhile.

'What's so special about teaching college jerks how to read books, anyway?'"

"Are you shitting me now? You're how old? About forty, right? You've got two kids and a lousy ex who's never going to let you go on with your life in peace, while he raises the boys for what, six years? Because that's how long it'll take before you're making a decent living."

"Jess, just because a teaching assistant doesn't make a hell of a lot of money doesn't mean I should forget about my dream. I have to start somewhere. We have no debts, good equity in the house, and his tenured professorship that more than pays the bills. I worked damned hard at jobs that were beneath me so he could advance his career. I know I've got two kids to mother. But it won't kill Eric to make a few sacrifices, if that's what you'd call it. He can come home early a few evenings to get a meal for the boys, get them into their showers, and put them to bed. I've gone the route of the supportive faculty wife, devoted mom, and community volunteer for years. I'm starved for my own life."

"I know how you feel, Kate. That's a good topic for next week's therapy."

"I'm finished with therapy, Jessica." Kate wondered if she did really need the group, for releasing the pressure valve.

"Whoa, Kate. This group is here exactly for these difficult times like you're having right now. I'm tired myself of showing up for therapy every week. I know group's good though. I blamed myself for the attack, like I'd tempted fate. I'd read the local papers. Nutcases are out there looking for someone like me. I'm still struggling with whether I was or wasn't the victim that night. I love hearing your story. Group has really helped me, and I don't want you to stop coming."

"You're right, Jessica. I'm just tired of thinking of others. Eric, the boys, my mother, my sisters . . . even having to listen to the rest of the group seems overwhelming right now. I still can't promise I'll come next week."

"At least promise you'll think about it."

Kate nodded, gave Jessica a hug, then got into her SUV. She watched to make sure Jessica safely reentered the building before driving off.

Kate felt full of uncertainty as she drove the Explorer through the local streets toward home, lost in thought. She had to gird herself for tomorrow—yet another Friday night visitation drama ahead.

Kate, worn down over and over by the war with Eric, hadn't the energy to fight for the court order that would enforce the boys' rights to choose whether or not they wanted go with Eric for weekend visitations. More time, more paperwork, and more money for her lawyer to draw up the documents and submit them. Not to mention explaining to the nosy neighbors why a local police officer had to be present when Eric arrived each week to pick up Josh and Ryan.

The look of hatred on Eric's face, as he waited each Friday night in the dimly lit background of the door outside her house, was unmistakable. It showed Kate their war was not over. In his arrogant way, anyone could tell who he thought would ultimately win this war.

On the weekends, when Josh and Ryan left with their father, hesitantly picking up their little red overnight bags, Kate would sit and cry. Just knowing how crazy Eric could be, Kate wondered, *how will I ever find a man who would be able to deal with me and my mad ex-husband in the background?*

It presented a topic she could envision herself talking over at the group therapy sessions. Maybe group could be a safety valve for her, part of her weekly routine, and an opportunity to vent her anger. Tonight her shame had been exposed.

During the ride home, Kate thought through the situation, looking for solutions. *I need to stop worrying about Eric's next hostile moves and start thinking about what to do for myself. Were Jessica's words about dating really that ludicrous? Tomorrow, I'm calling Liz. We can brainstorm together.*

Kate let a long sigh out slowly. Breathing again felt good. Kate opened the driver's side window and let the cold night air fill her lungs.

Chapter

Nine

Friday morning, Kate called Liz. A sleepy voice picked up on the fourth ring, right before the answering machine would record the call.

"Liz, I know it's early, but I've been awake all night, thinking and thinking. It's time for me to stop reacting to all of Eric's craziness. I need to focus on my own needs. My feelings . . ."

"Kid, that's what I've been trying to tell you. You've got to put yourself first. How're those wonderful boys of yours supposed to grow up feeling about women if their own mother is a teary-eyed, emotional wreck? You're a vibrant, very pretty, smart gal. If I see it, so will others. Give yourself a chance and get out there."

"Well, where do you feel I should start? It's been so long, I'm afraid I won't know how to handle the dating game anymore. Hell, I am a total blank here right now."

"My friend Susan—you know, the widow who lost her husband a couple of years ago—met someone at *Parents without Partners.*"

"Where and what is that? I am so out of the loop!"

"The nearest PWP is in Commack. That's where Susan met her fiancé last year. Susan said it's a very informal, nondrinking meetup. It doesn't mean getting all dressed up and doesn't matter whether you're single, divorced, or widowed. So just go!"

"Okay. I can Google PWP for directions. I'm sure glad to have a GPS in my SUV! "

Liz laughed and said goodbye.

Kate poured herself a cup of coffee, spread a bagel with cream cheese, and went into her home office. She Googled Parents without Partners. Sure enough, she had what she needed. The meetings were on Sunday nights from 7:30 to 9:00. Early enough. She could get Robin to babysit the boys and still be home before Robin's 10:00 curfew.

The boys would be at Eric's for the weekend, as stipulated in their separation agreement. Frank Collins, Kate's attorney had advised her not to pin herself down by having Eric take the boys every weekend, but Kate had not wanted Eric to say she'd prevented him from seeing his sons on a regular weekly basis. Now she was stuck with her decision. The weekends were lonely without the liveliness of Ryan and Josh. There were few places she could take them for amusement during the school week. Usually they went to the library or local park to kick a soccer ball around. Once they entered middle school, there would be more driving to after school activities—sports and such—maybe to a movie if there was a snow day.

Kate decided she would try to do some early Christmas shopping on Saturday afternoon at the Smith Haven Mall. These days, every kid wanted an iPad, Xbox, and cell phone. Gone were the days of playing board games and having playdates with other kids. At eleven years old, Ryan was getting near the age when he and his friends would be playing video games with friends online. Gone were the days of friends dropping in for after-school snacks and playing fun games in the backyard.

After two hours browsing around, going from one store to another, Kate's feet and spirit were exhausted. Time to go home, order in a pizza, and watch something on Roku, maybe a movie or a detective series. After all, tomorrow night was the PWP meeting.

Who knew what might come out of that?

Sunday night, Heather brought the boys back early, saying Eric had to grade test papers and needed the whole night to do it. They walked in calling for Kate.

Kate hollered out. "I'm upstairs having a shower."

The boys spoke to her through the bathroom door.

"On a Sunday night, Mom? What kind of meeting is on a Sunday night?"

"It's a grownups meeting, for parents. It starts at seven. Robin's coming over to babysit. You can watch a Netflix movie, make popcorn, whatever. But remember to take your showers. And get yourselves ready for school tomorrow. You know the routine. I'll be back by ten o'clock and check in on you both."

"But, Mom . . ."

"Enough, Ryan."

It was a frigid Sunday night, all right. Kate chose a multicolored cashmere sweater and pair of jeans, topped off with a shaggy white lambswool jacket, and finished off with her low-heeled boots. The weather report did mention the possibility of snow. Just as she finished getting ready, the doorbell rang.

"Hi, Robin. Thanks for coming tonight. I've already told the boys they can rent a movie and make some popcorn. Just, please, make sure they take their showers. Lights out at eight thirty. See you at ten . . ."

Kate wrapped a wool scarf around her neck, checked to make sure she had her keys in her shoulder handbag, and went out to the car. *Well, here's to my first singles adventure.*

When Kate entered the PWP meeting room, about twenty people were already seated on wooden chairs placed in rows. It looked like a school classroom. *Not a great beginning.* A woman briefly addressed the group, welcoming the newcomers. The first row of seats was mostly empty, except for a lone man, around her own age.

"Hi, I'm John Carlson."

"My name is Kate. Nice to meet you."

"This is your first meeting, right?"

"Yes, it is. One of my friends told me about it."

"Are you a widow or divorced?"

"I'm divorced."

"You aren't one of those Jericho Turnpike divorcees, are you?

"What is a Jericho Turnpike divorcee?"

"You know, the ones who go to all the bars on the Pike to meet men."

Kate frowned. It took her a moment to answer. "I have *never* done anything like that in my life!"

"Okay, sorry. I'm a widower myself. Lost my wife two years ago. Most of the women I've met do go to bars and hang out to meet men."

John had a sad story to tell of his late wife's losing battle with breast cancer. He was raising two little girls, six and eight years old. They compared notes about their kids and the difficulty of raising children as a single parent. Kate relaxed. *I think I could like this guy.*

"Kate, I would like to see you again."

"I feel the same way about you, John."

"How about meeting for dinner next Friday at the Steak and Stein Restaurant? It's kind of midway between where you live and where I live? It's a nice place, casual with good steaks. Unless you're a vegetarian?"

Kate laughed. "I'm probably one of the last carnivores on the planet these days!"

"Great. Is seven thirty a good time for you?"

"Mmm, yes. That would be fine."

"Let's exchange phone numbers, in case something comes up with one of the kids."

"Sure, I was thinking exactly the same thing."

They shook hands and left separately for each one's drive home.

Kate felt aglow. Looking in the rear-view mirror of the SUV, she saw her blushing cheeks and giggled. *Forty-three and I can still blush! Now, I'll actually have something to talk about in group on Thursday that doesn't involve Eric!*

Kate quickly went through her Monday morning routine: kids off to school, cash out of the ATM, groceries from the store, clothes dropped at the cleaners. She raced to get home to call Liz. *She'll get a kick out of boring old Kate about to step off into the dating world again!*

Kate reached home, threw her down jacket on a kitchen chair, and called her best buddy.

"Hi, Liz. I knew you'd finally answer," Kate said, after the phone rang six times at Liz's end. "I have something to tell you. Your hunch about PWP was just the push I needed."

"Tell me, friend. I actually think I'm hearing some excitement in your voice."

"I met a nice-looking guy, not a Ryan Gosling, but attractive and easy to talk to."

"And?"

"We have a date for dinner this Friday night at Steak and Stein!"

"Good for you! You sound excited, not like the 'Debbie Downer' I've become used to lately! What's his story?"

"His name is John Carlson. He's a widower with two young daughters. He works for Google in the City and commutes from Nassau County. The girls have a live-in who cares for them. He seems very organized—a housekeeper comes in twice a week. My only little nagging qualm is John seems a bit intense."

"Well, honey, you'll just have to see what that's about—after your date. But, Kate, I'm proud of you for taking the risk, finally."

"Well, that's my news of the day, Liz. I'll let you go. Talk to you before my therapy group, for sure."

"Great. Anyway, I'm off to get the last of my dental implants done tomorrow. God, it's taken forever. Too bad my dear parents never got me braces when I was a kid. I hate my overbite."

"You always look great to me. Now you'll look like a movie star—flashing a big grin all the time!"

"Stop will you! Bye!"

"Love you, Liz. And thanks again for the kick in the butt." Kate looked up at the kitchen wall where she kept the monthly calendar of appointments. Wednesday was the field trip with Ryan and his class to the art museum by bus. Not what she wanted to do in this freezing weather. Thursday night group. Friday date night! *Hope the busy week won't have my head fall into the soup bowl at the steakhouse.*

Group was nearly over, and Kate still hadn't had a chance to announce her news. She listened impatiently as Eden droned on. "I don't know why, but lately, Mother doesn't seem to want to come with me on Sunday to services. She says it's her fibromyalgia bothering her, but I'm not so sure. Maybe she's losing her faith. She's like you, Kate. After my father left, she swore off all men."

Kate burst out, impulsively. "Eden, I need to interrupt you this one time."

Joe sat with his arms crossed, looking hostile, but Kate went on. "I need to say something before the session is over: I have an actual *date* for dinner tomorrow night with someone I met."

Patsy let out a whoop. "You go, girl!"

"Yeah," said Jessica. "Remember, if this one's not for you, I can surely fix you up with one of Phil's lawyer pals."

The men in the group looked bored. Kate had nothing else to say, and the rest of the time ticked by.

Chapter

Ten

Kate dressed for her date with John. Knowing how severely critical he was about fast divorcees, Kate settled on a plain black long-sleeved wool dress, pearl earrings, and a simple gold chain for her neck. *Why do I feel like I'm wearing a costume?* She went light on the makeup and perfume and slung a pair of gold heels. *Kate, you dumb-ass people pleaser.*

Kate arrived a few minutes early and looked around at the tables of younger couples who were much more casually dressed in jeans and boots.

John was already waiting for Kate at the table he'd booked for their date. He wore a dark blue jacket, gray turtleneck sweater, and matching pants. Kate saw a slight smile cross his face, one of relief, when he saw Kate enter the restaurant.

He stood up, shook her hand. They exchanged hellos. She gave John a big smile and sat down.

"This is a cozy spot," Kate said, putting her elbows on the table.

The waitress came by soon after to take their drinks order. Kate decided to go with a dirty, dirty martini since Liz had said, "It'll really relax you, honey."

John ordered a beer.

The big fireplace, wood crackling, warmed Kate as much as her second drink did. John passed on a second drink and suggested they order their meals.

John's forehead showed lines Kate hadn't noticed at the PWP meeting. "So, John, how was your week?"

"Work is work, Kate."

"Well, I'm just interested. I'm a regular Google user. It's like a know-it-all best friend. You'd be surprised at all the things—"

"I work at the development center in Manhattan. I don't program answers. I thought you understood that."

"So, . . . let's just leave it at that, I guess."

Kate's stumbling conversation was relieved by the waitress setting down their sizzling steak platters before them. "God, I didn't realize I was this hungry. The food looks great, John."

"You must have raised an appetite after your two martinis. I don't care for hard liquor myself."

Kate shifted in her chair. "I don't have a drinking problem, John, if that is what you're thinking."

"To be honest with you, my wife never drank anything stronger than an Arnold Palmer in the summer or Earl Grey tea with cream during the winter. Her world revolved around me and the girls."

"Well, she sounds like quite a gal. I can see you miss her very much."

The waitress came by again. "Anything else you folks would like to order? More bread? Another drink?"

John's irritable look silenced the waitress, and she walked away from their table.

"Yes, Beth was our world. Frankly, Kate, I'm not out to date casually. I'm looking for the right woman. One who'll be like another mother to my daughters."

"Oh, I see, John. I guess you and I have two different agendas. I'm already a mother to my two sons, totally. I can't even begin to think about raising anyone else's kids. She let out a sigh. "Sorry to disappoint you, but you deserve the truth. You're a very nice family guy. I respect that. Really, I do. I hope you find the right woman."

The waitress brought their check. John paid it and helped Kate on with her camel wool coat. She put on her gloves. They walked silently to her car. He opened the door for Kate, who slid in behind the wheel.

"Good night, John. Safe drive home."

"Same to you, Kate."

On the drive back to her house, Kate thought over the evening's outcome.

That was a real bust of your first dating balloon. Guess it's time to talk to Jess about a date with one of Phil's lawyer pals . . . I'm proud of myself. Like the sculptor, Louise Nevelson once said, or so I remember from that TV program about her: "I will not be defeated." If I can keep dealing with Eric, I can keep on dating until I meet someone right for me.

Kate got out of the car, walking quickly in the frigid night air.

"Hi, Robin, Kate called out. I'm back." Kate spoke to Robin about the boys and took care of her pay. It was late, but Kate knew Liz would still be up when she got her on her cell phone.

"Liz. Ugh! Ugly night."

"Oy! What happened with Mr. John Nice Guy?"

"He's not looking for dates. He's looking for a substitute mother for his saintly dead wife's daughters."

"He said that, literally?"

"Not those exact words, but he made it clear. And he acted as if I were an alcoholic because I ordered two dirty, dirty martinis to his one beer. One. A woman who drinks hard liquor is not second mother potential."

"So sorry. What's next, honey?"

"Well, this coming Thursday is our next-to-last therapy group until after the New Year. I'm thinking of having Phil get me a date with one of his lawyer pals after all. Hopefully, the one Jess says looks like a young Robert Redford!"

"Good idea. I guess you'll 'share' this lousy PWP date with the group?"

"You got that right. As Scarlett O'Hara liked saying, I won't think about that tonight. I'll think about it tomorrow, or something like that."

"At least you've got a plan and you're not blubbering about this lost opportunity for a future relationship. I know you too well, Kate, my girl."

"You're so on target with my mind, Liz, you scare me sometimes!"

On Monday, after the boys left for school, Kate called Jessica.

"Kate! I hoped you'd call. I've been wondering about you. How'd your date go?"

"It was a bust, Jess. Please keep this to yourself; it's not for the group—but I've thought it over and would like Phil to set me up with one of his colleagues for a date."

"Yay! There are a few of the guys I think you'd have fun dating. I'll talk to Phil when he gets home tonight. Call you tomorrow for sure, Kate. I know something will work out."

"Great. Thanks. I'm groaning a bit about telling the group about my abortive experience last night."

"What happened? Talk to me."

Kate smiled to herself. "Got to save some things for our beloved group meeting. Otherwise, you'd be bored twice!"

Tuesday, Jess called Kate, excitement in her voice, she nearly cackled out her successful talk with Phil. "Phil's got a friend named Gary who's interested in meeting you. He gave Gary a great spiel about you. So, expect a call."

"Is Gary the Redford clone?"

"Nah. But he's tall, nice build, and has a fun sense of humor. And he's kind of cute."

"You did good, mama. Really, thanks, Jess. See you on Thursday. Hope Gary does call. I don't want to lose my confidence after just one lousy evening out."

"Good girl! Bye."

Chapter

Eleven

Thursday rolled around. The second to the last meeting of the year. Kate had been rehearsing in her head as to how much to share with the group about her wasted date night with John. Frankly, Kate had already had her fill of sharing.

Feeling like a grumpy kid who didn't get what she'd wanted for Christmas, Kate tried not to be disappointed when a call from Gary didn't materialize all week. Gary could still call before the year ended. The holiday season was hectic for everybody. *Boy can I ever rationalize everything!*

Kate said goodnight to the boys, who were already preoccupied with showing Robin their latest game. She came down the stairs dressed elegantly in a cashmere sweater and pants, pulled on fur-lined high-heeled boots, threw a warm wool coat over her outfit, wrapped a red plaid scarf around her throat, tugged cashmere-lined red gloves on her ice-cold fingers, and walked quickly to her car. It was freezing inside. She turned on the heater, and a blast of cold air hit her at once. Luckily, the Explorer's heater worked fast and she warmed up quickly on the drive.

A bright flush came into her cheeks as she entered the low-lit room where the group met. Looked like she was the last to arrive. When she walked in, all in the group turned to look at her. She wondered if she had been the topic of conversation.

As soon as Kate sat down, Vinnie started the meeting. "Who wants to go first?" Vinny asked, looking around the room.

"I will."

Okay, Kate, you're on."

"Here we go again," groaned Joe. "What's this week's install-ment of *Eric the Terrible.*"

"Sorry to disappoint you, Joe. But I'm not going there." I had a wholesome but boring dinner date with a nice guy I met at a Parents Without Partners group in Commack. The only drawback is that he was looking for a substitute mother for his two young kids."

"Another loser divorced guy, right?"

"No, Joe, he's a widower. His wife died two years ago of breast cancer. He and the girls are lost without her. I'm disappointed, but not depressed about it. It was just a new experience, that's all. I'm holding myself together, thanks to this group."

"That's really nice to hear, Kate." Vinny looked around the room. "Remember the exercise we did when we first started group?"

Rhoda piped up. "I do. You had us all stand up with our legs planted firmly apart on the floor."

Pete remembered and said, "No matter what happens, my feet will hold me up."

Dan nodded his agreement. "Sometimes, when I feel helpless, that becomes my mantra."

"Come off that bullshit, Pete. It sounds like politically correct crap to me!"

"Joe, I feel sorry for you. What do you have to rely on for com-fort, anyway?" Rhoda said.

"Rhoda, I can take care of myself without saying some mumbo jumbo."

"You call having three failed marriages taking care of yourself? I don't think you've learned anything about your inner self!"

"The mouse finally roars! Score one for Little Miss Perfect!

Patsy leaned across Eden and hissed at Joe. "Shut the fuck up, will you? You never let anyone in, you're so guarded. Here it is, almost Christmas, and you are just like Scrooge. With you, everything's bah humbug, except it's all year round.

"Speaking of the holidays," Vinny said, breaking the tension in the room, "does anyone care to share what his or her plans are before we finish for the night?"

Each person answered, some saying a few words, others too much detail.

There was a hesitant silence. "Well, then, I guess that ends this week's therapy session. Personally, my hope is that you all find some peace in your hearts. We've had our share of drama. This is the season for some joy. I hope you all find that in your own way."

"No group hug, Vinny?"

"Only if everyone agrees, Eden."

"Nah," said Joe. "Save it till next week."

Slowly, everyone stood up in somewhat uncomfortable positions around each other. Kate crossed the room, hugged Patsy and Jess. "Merry pre-Christmas to all of us." She saw Vinny smile.

"Same time. Same place. Next week!" Vinnie said.

Everyone nodded, shambling out of the room, each lost in thought.

Patsy caught up with Kate before she made it out the door. Officially separated from the husband of their three kids, Patsy asked Kate to go out with her Saturday night. This was against Dr. Rossetti's rules of outside contact, but Kate said yes. The last date had acted as an emotional release valve, even if it did go badly. It had been the antidote to Eric's increasing hostility and denigration of her as a desirable woman.

Chapter

Twelve

Kate and Patsy met up on Saturday night. They went, at Pat's suggestion, to a singles bar in the next county.

Kate immediately felt attracted to a handsome blond, a younger guy. She smiled brightly at him, lowering her gaze in a flirty way. He walked over to Kate, a tall glass of beer in his hand.

"Hi, my name's Tommy. What's yours?"

"I'm Kate."

"Nice name for a nice-looking person."

Kate felt flush. Was it the from the heat of the crowded bar room, or from him?

"Buy you a drink, Kate?"

"Sure. I'll have cranberry and vodka, please."

"You got it."

Kate watched Tommy's smooth walk through the crowded bar. After a short wait, he returned with her drink. Kate nearly gulped the drink, stopping partway through to squeeze the slice of lime into the vodka.

"Live around here?"

"No. In Stony Brook."

"Lot of fancy folks out there."

"Well, my ex teaches at SUNY.

"Single myself. My buddy Nick and I share an apartment near here. We're in the construction business. Done some work on the hospital in Stony Brook. Minor stuff, though."

"Well, you sure look strong enough to be a builder."

"Yeah, gotta be. You look like you're about ready for a refill. Want another?"

"Guess I'm thirstier than I thought." *What am I doing? I'm getting buzzed is what I'm doing!* "Sure, that'll be great, Tommy."

When he returned with their drinks, Tommy stood closer to Kate. His blue eyes looking into hers made her body feel warm.

Their talk was light-hearted and easy in the noisy barroom.

Patsy came over with a guy she'd been having drinks with. She introduced him as Sean. "Having fun?"

"We sure are. Kate is an interesting person to talk to. But you probably already know that!"

Patsy smiled. "I like Donnegan's. Don't you, Kate?"

"I'm having fun here, Patsy."

After they ordered another drink and chatted awhile, Patsy said to Kate, "Sean's gonna take me home now, Kate. Will you be all right to drive home?"

"I'd be happy to take you, Kate," Tommy said without hesitation.

"Very nice of you, Tommy."

They said goodbye to Patsy and Sean. Tommy asked Kate if she was ready for another drink. "No, thank you, Tommy. Those three drinks went straight to my brain! I'm ready to head for home."

Before they left Donnegan's, Tommy asked for Kate's phone number. Feeling the effects of the alcohol, plus her attraction to him, Kate said it was fine with her. Tommy took down her number on a bar napkin and put it in a pocket of his black leather jacket. She asked for Tommy's in return, so she'd know who it was when the phone rang.

"It sure is cold out," Kate said as she stepped outside into snow flurries.

"December. What can you say?"

"I'm glad you're driving, Tommy, and not me." Kate giggled.

It didn't take long before Tommy's first phone call. She saw the number and hesitated as to whether she should pick up or not—torn between fascination and fear, a sexy glow and physical longing.

She answered, and right away he asked her out.

"I'd like that very much, Tommy."

They decided on dinner at one of Kate's favorite restaurants in Port Jefferson. Casual setting, good food, near home.

Kate's imagination raced in anticipation of her coming dinner date with Tommy.

Chapter

Thirteen

Tommy picked Kate up at eight o'clock, and they drove the short distance to the restaurant. Kate enjoyed everything about the evening.

Heading out of the restaurant, Tommy surprised Kate with his direct approach. "Kate, I feel very attracted to you," he said.

"You must be a mind reader, Tommy."

"Would you like to go somewhere else instead of straight home?"

"It's nice down by the wharf. We could walk there. It's pretty close by."

The scent of the Long Island Sound water, the feel of Tommy's arm around her shoulder, all felt wonderful. The night sky was clear and bright. "I feel so relaxed, Tommy. Don't you?"

"Mmm. Yes, I do."

"Let's not leave yet."

"What do you want to do, Kate?"

"I feel totally intoxicated by everything tonight."

"Then let's not go."

"It's a wonderful thought, Tommy. But I have to get home for the kids. My sitter has a curfew."

"I understand, but I want to see you again, Kate."

"Sure. I'd like that, Tommy."

They passed a quaint motel, one of several for visitors who came to Port Jefferson by ferry each day to sightsee and stay overnight. Kate felt a deep, warm, sexual sensation.

"There's a real temptation," Kate said, pointing to the motel.

"You could always call your sitter."

"No, I can't."

"Aw, c'mon, Kate. You can call the sitter, and we'll get a room on the next block, by the water."

Kate's body ached. She looked into Tommy's sea-blue eyes, feeling she might explode with desire for his body on hers. Kate's fingers tingled as she held the cell phone close to her ear.

Robin picked up, sounding sleepy.

Kate made the pitch.

"I guess I could stay, but just for an hour."

Tommy's smile was triumphant. Kate was caught on his line.

Kate felt she might explode. The sexual release was so healing. They made it home in the promised hour, lingering over long, deep kisses in Kate's driveway, and then they parted.

Chapter

Fourteen

Before the last therapy session of the year, Kate called Patsy. "I've been having a good time with Tommy this week. For the first time since I threw Eric out, I feel like a desirable woman again."

Patsy thought the story was thrilling. Kate had done the unexpected thing and gone off with a near stranger to screw in a motel.

"So, you'll be seeing Tommy again for some more magical sex?"

"No, he's too slick for me. Tommy was just my 'zipless fuck.'"

"Well, you have a lot of stuff to share at tonight's session, at least! See you there soon."

Everyone took their usual seats in the therapy room at seven thirty.

"I'm going to tell you all about the new me," Kate said, starting out. "I met a guy, and we've had a few terrific dates together. I feel like a desirable woman, not a helpless, boring old shoe."

"Kate you don't want to become like Eric. It's not the Christian way of behaving. Don't sink to his level."

"Rhoda, it's natural to have these desires. I just don't know if I'm ready to commit to more yet."

Eden nodded.

"What have you three guys to say about Kate's feelings?"

Joe jumped right in with his opinion. "Vinny, if Kate was my wife and I found out about what she was doing, I'd probably beat the shit out of her! Kate and that Tommy guy in a one-night stand at some seedy motel. He might have been a crazy son-of-a-bitch and killed her!"

Pete had a different take. "You got to be careful who you get hooked up with. You don't want to get mixed up with somebody you don't really know. My wife was a lousy drunk, always blaming me for not giving her a better life. Half the time, though, she would lie in bed, too hung over to feed the baby. I would have to give him a bottle, change his diaper, and leave him in his crib with two or three more bottles of milk before I left for my construction job. Sherry was a hopeless mental case who was also an alky. It got so bad, I was afraid I would cause serious damage to someone's installation on site."

Dan, too, had a story. "Laura cheated on me whenever I was out of town on an insurance fraud case. A couple of anonymous phone calls finally clued me in."

Kate's heart sank listening to the anger and distrust. No wonder these guys had not been supportive of her. They thought of themselves as victims in their relationships. They had little sympathy for her newfound freedom.

Chapter

Fifteen

Kate was glad the therapy group was behind her, for this year at least. Now she could let the excitement of Christmas wash over her. She put on her holiday snowman scenic sweater and red-and-green plaid pants and went out to do the last of her present buying. Kate had tickets to the Westbury Music Center for the holiday show. The boys would enjoy the *Santa's Christmas at the North Pole* production. Last year's Cub Scout trip to see *The Nutcracker* had been a big bust! No sugar plum fairies dancing for her boys.

She stopped in at a local boutique and bought herself a slinky silver-gray jersey dress with a side slit. A pair of four-inch designer heels in red and gray trimmed suede caught her eye. Just right for Liz's New Year's party.

The one downer, and it was a big one, was Eric's having Ryan and Josh for the entire Christmas holiday this year. Kate regretted having agreed to the provision in their separation agreement concerning Christmas and Easter holidays. Each parent would get to have the boys on alternate years.

What'll I do without Josh and Ryan? I don't know if I can handle this splitting of holiday visitations. Thanksgiving sure didn't go well for me.

Kate put her purchases in the SUV and sat silently in the driver's seat. Tears began to form in her eyes. After a short crying session, she checked herself in the rear-view mirror. *I look lousy . . . Next I'm buying waterproof mascara.* She dabbed at her smeared, puffy eyes with a tissue.

Kate felt pleased at her purchases of the latest Harry Potter book, *The Wind in the Willows,* and *The Lion, the Witch and the Wardrobe* for Josh. She knew Ryan would love the rock tumbler and remote-controlled drone. The Xbox they could share. Presents were only a small part of their holiday traditions.

Thinking back on Christmas memories, she knew one tradition would have to be scuttled from now on. As a family, the four of them would go to a neighboring Christmas tree farm to cut down their annual tree. This was probably their happiest time together, a hunt to find the most perfectly shaped, tallest tree. The smell of the evergreen trees and wreaths excited them all. Eric would tie the tree to the SUV's roof. They would drive home singing Christmas carols, feeling frozen but happy, looking forward to setting it up in the high-ceilinged living room. Kate would put on Christmas music and make cocoa, Eric would string lights, and they all would decorate the tree with ornaments, tinsel, and silvery garland.

Kate decided to treat herself to a peppermint mocha from Starbucks before heading home to wrap the boys' Christmas gifts. At Starbucks, she ran into her neighbor Debbie. They exchanged hellos.

"How are you spending Christmas, Kate?"

"Looks like I'm by myself this year. Eric will have the boys at his place, and I'm not feeling up to heading to my sister's family gathering alone. How about you?"

"Pretty much the story. What if we went out for Christmas dinner together?"

"I don't think any place will be open."

"There's the *The Hot Wok.* Chinese restaurants are always open on Christmas. I went there the first year Larry and I were separated—food's pretty decent, too."

"Okay. Sounds good to me. Better than crying into my eggnog!"

"Good. I'll pick you up."

"I'll supply a bottle of champagne!"

"Sure, Egg Foo Yung and champagne—a great combo!"

For her last stop, Kate had bought an oversized, ornately decorated, fresh evergreen wreath to hang on the front door. It would be a welcoming sight.

Kate reached home feeling stronger. Tossing her coat over a kitchen stool, she lit up a cigarette—too bad she couldn't break that nasty habit—then turned on the Braun coffeemaker and listened as the machine dripped the ground coffee. She drank two mugs with the usual cream plus a cube of demerara sugar while she hung up her wreath and wrapped the boys' gifts.

Chapter

Sixteen

In the midst of feeling more at ease with the upcoming holidays, Kate was brought back to reality by the upcoming appointment with her lawyer. All the weekly drives to her lawyer's office in Huntington were taking their toll on her. Even therapy was not as traumatic. Every time she agreed with one of Eric's demands, he would get suspicious of her motives, and another quarrel would result, followed by more pages being added to the ever-lengthening separation agreement.

"Thank God for your steady support, Frank," Kate said, sitting in front of his large office desk. He was the source of priestly advice. At first Kate had wanted Eric back.

"What would you be getting from that, Kate?" Frank ran his hand across his desk in an agitated way. His brown suit looked rumpled and his tie protruded on his middle-aged paunch, but he was terrific anyway. "Believe me, the man has no morals. A couple of years from now, you'd be sitting here in my office with three kids to protect. I could get him back, but for what? What normal father puts into a legal document that he knows one of his sons is not his? Suppose Ryan or Josh ever saw that in print? Eric's a disgusting excuse for a husband and father."

Kate sighed deeply. She found it so painful to remember Eric's crazy accusation about the boys' paternity. There was no end to his wacko "theories." At one point, he thought maybe Josh wasn't his, but no, "Josh looks like me." Then it was Ryan who had suspicious parentage, an accusation answered by a fellow colleague of Eric's who said, "Ryan has all your same mannerisms."

Continuing, Frank said, "You know with all the #MeToo sexual harassment charges floating around these days, maybe we could use Eric's affair with the physics department secretary against him. We might be able to get him fired on a morals clause. She may be angry enough by Eric's dumping of her, after her cancer and an abortion, that she might be willing to testify against Eric in a morals case.

"She might. But I'm kind of skeptical about it. I think she's still infatuated with him, crazy as it sounds." Kate also recalled Eric's divorce attorney, Sam Rolfe, a forty-something, short, sweaty, bloated lawyer. She despised meeting with Rolfe. He would pace back and forth in Frank's office, with his greasy dark hair in need of a haircut, gleefully laying out his next move against Kate. She felt nauseated thinking of having to meet again with this troll of a man to finalize the separation agreement before she and Eric went to court for the divorce. His seedy office on top of a household finance company only added to the overall picture of the kind of lawyer Kate hoped never to encounter.

Back in the spring, Kate had sat at the conference table wearing a simple vanilla-colored short-sleeved sweater and beige pants. She wore coral lipstick and matching blush to give her pale face some color. Eric had looked her over, smirking. Surprisingly, he looked upbeat, wearing a light blue sport shirt, open at the neck, dark gray pants, and loafers. Eric kept himself in good shape through tennis matches played with the same friendly rival every other day. Kate gave Eric a wan smile as she settled herself in a comfortable chair in Frank's office.

Rolfe, in his bombastic way, had wasted no time in harassing Kate. He looked like an angry Rottweiler. "You'd better give your husband what he wants in the divorce, or I will advise my client to go to the Dominican Republic, and you will get nothing!" Rolfe demanded she turn over her credit cards. Frank nodded so as to say she had no choice and needed to do so. Rolfe proceeded to cut them all up in front of her, in front of Eric, who didn't say a word.

Kate shook and burst out crying, feeling like a little kid being punished for something she hadn't done wrong. Frank brought her a box a tissue and patted her shoulder in comfort. He ended the meeting with authority. "That's enough for today, Rolfe. Kate and I have things to go over."

The whole drive home she had berated herself for looking weak in front of Eric and Rolfe. Kate, still in a fog, had called Liz. "I can't believe how weak I looked in there. Sobbing, frightened. Eric just sat there, enjoying it all. He looked so at ease. His face was tanned. He was in good physical shape. He bragged about his upcoming resort vacation, since his classes were over for the semester. To top it off, his teeny-tiny, adoring girlfriend was waiting for him in the parking lot. He has all that, and what do I have?"

"You have your boys," Liz said.

"The boys, yes. Thank God for them. But I also have late support checks and mounting debts, a boring routine of endless tasks, and no one to comfort me."

That night, to her surprise, Eric had come to the front door, a sheepish look on his face. "Don't worry about what Rolfe said in there, that Dominican Republic thing. I won't let that happen to you. He told me he loves destroying the wife's credit cards and making them cry."

"What a bastard. But isn't that why you chose him, Eric?"

After Kate had more time to collect her thoughts, she decided on a plan of her own.

"All the credit cards are in my name, not Eric's," she said to Liz. That thought made her laugh out loud.

Kate contacted each department store and credit card company. "I've lost my credit card. Could you please issue me a new one?"

Within a week, Kate had them all back. Her first purchase was for four auto tires and a tune-up.

"I think I'm ready for a tune up myself," she said to Liz. They had agreed to book a spa appointment and start the new year off right.

Chapter

Seventeen

N ew Year's Eve came, and that meant Liz and Mitch's celebration. Kate was still in a funk, too long alone in a too quiet house. She had no plans, except for this invitation to join Liz and other friends to ring in the New Year.

Dressing in her new slinky, jersey dress with the outrageously high-heeled shoes made her feel sexier. After her recent dating experiences with exciting, but dangerous, Tommy—and then Phil's friend Gary, who'd bored her nearly to death—Kate decided not to ask Jess or Patsy for any new date recommendations.

Kate was going to go to Liz's New Year's Eve party solo, hoping an unattached, "normal" guy might catch her eye.

Their house was a Christmas pageant of lights, with evergreen branches elegantly arranged on top of the fireplace and the hugest Christmas tree Kate had seen in years, all done up with Liz's artistic flair. Instead of colored lights and the usual accompaniments on the tree, Liz had shimmering silver bells sprinkled with artificial snow and antique miniature sleds hanging delicately from the tree's long green branches. The living room bustled with well-dressed friends of the couple. In the center of a table sat a punchbowl, filled not with eggnog but with Long Island Iced Tea.

"A few ladlesful of that," Kate said to Liz after tasting a cupful, "and you could take out my appendix without anesthesia."

"That's the idea, sugarplum."

Liz hoped the party would lighten Kate's spirits and bring a freshness to her life. She toasted for "a fresh start for the new year." Liz served cockles and mussels, delicately and expertly prepared and presented to the guests. Gourmet cheeses, pâté, and caviar were served in dishes on top of holly boughs on an extension table that stretched the length of the entire dining room. Kate poured herself another cup of the potent Long Island Tea. A lightly warm, relaxing feeling was beginning.

"I'm definitely going to enjoy myself," she said to Liz.

"I'll make some introductions."

"That's okay. I'll mingle."

Kate walked slowly about the living room, drink in hand, smiling as real as she could manage. She looked for an approachable person with whom to have an opening conversation. She said her "Hi, I'm Kate, Liz's friend," with as much brightness she could manage.

One male faculty member showed interest, told her about his research, then asked, "What do you do?"

She felt like the creature in *Alice in Wonderland* who smoked from a hookah, acting blasé about it all. Kate's eyes widened. *I'm a miserable soon-to-be-divorcee raising two children at home with no job . . . No, not tonight . . . I'm a sexy lady out for one hell of a holiday bash.*

"What do I do, you asked? I try to have a much fun as I can, to live in the moment, not for a paycheck, and explore what it means to be me."

The owlish guy moved on.

"No fucking sense of humor there," Kate mumbled. She kept on looking and smiling, feeling no pain, thanks to the potent drinks she'd already downed.

She talked to many of the guests, sharing equally inebriated jokes, complimenting Liz on the artistry of the decorations and creativity of the feast she had so marvelously pulled together.

After the ritual champagne toast at midnight, Kate sang *Auld Lang Syne* along with the group. The night was one of funny toasts and friendly kisses. The party was still rocking to music at two in the morning. And Kate's new heels were burning her feet.

Sensing the party was breaking up, Kate dug out her white lambswool coat from the pile on the guest bed and prepared to leave.

Liz met Kate at the door. "Better times will come, Kate. It's a new year, and there's always hope in a new year."

Kate smiled at Liz's optimistic outlook. "Liz, I had a great time tonight. Really. I felt relaxed and happy being here with your pals. And the tea certainly sealed the deal!"

"Whatever works, I always say. You know I've always got your back, honey. Call you tomorrow." Kate kissed Liz on the cheek and walked out into the cold night air.

Kate hugged her coat to her as the icy wind hit her face.

Chapter

Eighteen

As the weather slowly turned from winter to spring, the weekly drives to her lawyer's office became easier. Dealings with Eric remained tense.

One day, he appeared in the kitchen. "I want to take the boys for the whole summer. Of course, since I'd be having them, I wouldn't send you support checks for those months."

Kate was shocked to see him and tried to gather her thoughts for a response that wouldn't set off his anger. "Eric, bills for the house still have to be paid. I need those checks."

Eric smirked. "Then get yourself a summer job."

Kate gave an answer to get Eric out of the house. "Let me think about it. Summer is still a way off."

Early that evening, the phone rang. Heather's eighteen-year-old baby voice sounded frantic. "Kate, I'm afraid if you don't let Eric have the boys for the summer, he will take them away forever, and you'll never see them again."

"Hang on a minute here, Heather. Eric wouldn't jeopardize his job at the university by doing anything erratic, or illegal."

"I'm just telling you to be careful. The other morning, when I went out to my car, there were black feathers on the hood. Lourdes, my neighbor, told me that in her culture black feathers mean danger, even death—it was a warning sign, Lourdes said."

Kate knew Eric was becoming more unstable. Anything was possible. Josh had already come home from the previous weekend's visitation with Eric telling her a story that chilled her to her core.

"Daddy told us there was a divorced man who killed his ex-wife, his kids, and then himself when he couldn't have the kids to himself."

"Document everything. The threats, crazy talk, everything," Kate's lawyer advised. "We may need to get you an order of protection before this case is over. This guy is a total Looney Tune."

Kate carried on, taking the dog to the vet, the boys to their play dates. Living her life as calm as she could.

Friday's mail greeted Kate with an envelope bearing "Mt. Everest" as the return address. Kate ripped it open and pulled out the overdue child-support check. Another joke of Eric's. The postmark read Los Angeles, the hometown of one of Eric's recent girlfriends, a math teacher who had been finishing her sabbatical at the same Long Island university at which Eric had taught. She was now teaching at USC. Kate almost felt sorry for the dumb, childlike misfit who thought she was Eric's forever girl.

Chapter

Nineteen

In early April, Liz and Kate met for a late breakfast. Kate had a one o'clock meeting at Frank's office. Liz was going shopping for a new Easter outfit to wear to her mother-in-law's Easter dinner later that week. Liz was in a great mood, breezing into the little café in Stony Brook.

"I just love Easter, even without having kids. I love volunteering at the halfway house, coloring Easter eggs, making baskets for presents—and this year, I'm dressing up in an Easter Bunny suit! How's that for fun? What about you? Tell me about your plans."

"I haven't made plans. I'm beginning to think this divorce thing will never get settled. Always more paperwork, more meetings, more fighting over every dotted 'i' and crossed 't.'"

"I'm sorry, Kate. You're obviously feeling very glum."

Kate confided, "Going to my lawyer's office every week has become my church, like going to Mass. I do the same thing every week. That and saying goodbye to the kids every Friday. The kids are reluctant to go with Eric. I practically have to force them to leave with him. As soon as I pack up their overnight bags, Josh starts getting a stomachache. It's on to round two: getting a court order so they don't have to go if they don't want to. To top it off, Eric is writing embarrassing things on his support checks, like 'the boys need new shoes.' I deposit them electronically these days so I don't have to face the bank tellers."

Liz said, "Honey, take the damn checks to his bank to get cashed. Then he'll be embarrassed for the asshole he is!"

Kate and Liz went to the local diner for lunch on a somewhat balmy April Saturday after Easter was over. Liz ordered a Cobb salad. "Got to take off some Christmas and Easter pounds." Kate ordered comfort food: cheeseburger, onion rings, a large Coke.

"Kate, it's time for me to step up my efforts to put some joy back in your life. You are dealing with a 'mad scientist.' And that's no joke."

"I'm thankful to have you, my lawyer, and weekly therapy."

"I know how you feel about blind dates, but I know a really nice, mellow divorced guy I'd like you to meet."

"Not another lawyer, I hope."

"As matter of fact, he is. Mitch and I have known Jake for years. Believe me, he's stable and has a great sense of humor, to boot. He lives just a few blocks away from you. Let me give Jake your number. C'mon."

"You got me in a weak moment. I'm starved, and not just for that cheeseburger and fries coming our way!"

Chapter

Twenty

Two weeks passed without a call from Jake. Kate took it philosophically. If it happened, it happened. Either way, she could deal with it.

Then, on Wednesday night, the phone rang. A pleasant male voice spoke her name. "Hi, Kate, our mutual friend, Liz, gave me your number a while back. Sorry it took me so long to call, but I had a court case that took a long time to settle."

"I'm fine with that, Jake. I've been busy entertaining my sons. We've been enjoying the early beach weather."

"Speaking of beaches, how would you feel about having dinner with me on Saturday night at the Stony Brook Inn?"

"It's one of my favorite restaurants, Jake. I'd love to go with you."

"What time should I make our reservation?"

"Eight o'clock would be perfect for me."

"Sounds great to me, Kate."

Thursday, Kate walked into group therapy in a happy state of mind. The group took notice. Jessica smiled, turned to Kate, nodded, and said, "What's up with you tonight? You seem happy. No Eric drama to report?"

"I am in a good place at the moment. A friend set up a date for me. We're going out for dinner on Saturday. As for Eric, he hasn't spoken again about taking the boys for the summer. He's been busy hunting with dopey for a condo."

Dan smiled. "I'm glad for you, Kate. It's taken a long time for me to trust a woman again, but I've been seeing a wonderful woman. She's also divorced, with a young daughter. We've only been going together for a couple of months, so I didn't think I was ready to share it with the group, but I feel it's leading to something really special."

Joe's sneer startled Dan. "Some guys never learn," he said. "Women put on a good act until you're hooked. Never knew one who was what she seemed."

Shy Eden spoke up. "Joe, you've been married three times. You must have had a part in some of your troubles. We all have flaws, after all. Maybe if you had some sort of spiritual belief you might find more contentment."

"Ha! You're still living with mommy and daddy. What has God done for you? No husband; no kids . . ."

"No Joe, you're wrong. I had a fiancé about ten years ago. We were close to getting married. His car went off an icy road in Connecticut one night and rolled down an embankment. When he died, I lost my one great love. I found solace in my church. I became a deacon, bringing Mass to the elderly and shut-ins. You may laugh, but it has been a great blessing to me. Now, my worry is how to take the best care of my elderly parents. I was a late-in-life baby. My parents are both ailing. I need to be strong to cope with their decline and my loss to come. That's my reason for being in group."

Vinny felt the tension in the room and steered the meeting's direction for the time remaining. When the group's time came to an end, everyone left, not speaking directly to one another.

Only Jessica stopped to wish Kate good luck with her date with Jake. They hugged and said goodnight.

Chapter

Twenty One

Saturday night, date night, rolled around. Robin came early to play video games with Josh and Ryan. Kate put on her little black dress with spaghetti straps, old reliable.

She felt great, freshly made up, ready for a good dinner and grownup conversation with a promising date. They had arranged to meet at the Inn, separately.

Kate entered the restaurant and watched a tall, dark-haired, smiling man around her age come toward her.

"How did you know it was me," Kate asked.

"Liz gave me a pretty good description of you." Jake smiled. "Besides, all the older folks have already left!"

A cute young waiter took their drinks order and returned with their cocktails within minutes. Looking over the menu, they decided to share broiled oysters as an appetizer, followed by meals of herb-crusted halibut paired with a bottle of chardonnay.

Conversation flowed as easily as the wine. Jake, also divorced, had joint custody of a seven-year-old daughter, Lily, who lived with his ex-wife. All in all, it was the relaxed evening Kate had been hoping it would be.

Jake walked Kate to her car, brushing her cheek with a friendly kiss. Closing the car door, he asked her if he could see her the following Saturday night. Kate smiled and said yes.

She would have to call Liz to thank her for the delightful introduction to this normal, mature man.

Chapter

Twenty Two

Kate sat facing her lawyer after the hour-long drive to reach his office. She heard herself confiding more than he probably wanted to hear. "My nerves feel shot. I've lost over thirty pounds in five months because I smoke more than I eat."

Frank looked genuinely concerned. "That's not a good situation for you or the boys. You need to look your best, be your best, when you come in front of the judge. I want you on the top of your game when you walk into divorce court."

"I don't really think I even care about the divorce. My neighbor told me a story about how she made her husband wait a year before she'd sign the divorce papers. In that year, Maddie's husband realized what he had done, he changed. Now they're together again, and they're happy!"

"Kate, not this again. You're forgetting, I know Eric. You've got to stop thinking about saving this marriage and start thinking about saving yourself. I can get Eric back to you, but he is totally amoral. If he were to return to you, you would have to deal with his infidelity all over again. We need to fight this head on, Kate. Rolfe is the type of lawyer we call a 'bomber.' This guy goes for the spouse's jugular, and loves doing it."

Chapter

Twenty Three

Because Eric and Kate jointly owned the house she and the boys still lived in, Eric had carte blanche to enter. He found small ways to intrude on her and keep her constantly on edge. He played both an offensive and a defensive game, accusing her of tapping his phone and having him followed. Some weekends, he would not come for Ryan and Josh until his actual visiting time was over. One time, he stood on the porch after being denied entry and put his fists through the French doors, shattering glass everywhere. Then he went through the house calling for the boys, saying daddy was taking them out to go buy toys.

The torment escalated as Eric worked nonstop to wear Kate down. When Kate returned from the grocery store one morning after dropping off the kids, she saw a taxi in the driveway. Inside the house, Eric had piled up the computer, two TVs, her great-grand-mother's candlesticks, and her private diaries, taken from her dresser drawer.

Kate yelled, "What are you doing, Eric?"

He didn't pay any attention to anything she said. Racing out the back door, he got into her car, which still had the keys in the ignition, and sped away. As he drove off, so did the taxi driver, who must have either been paid to wait or recognized his fare had just ditched him. If it wasn't bad enough that he had raced off with a week's supply of groceries, he'd done so on her carpool day.

In a frantic daze, Kate began running down the street toward a neighbor's house. Nobody was home. She tried banging on the door of three other homes. Finally, a neighbor she didn't know answered the door. "Please help me. I live just down the street. My car's been stolen, and I must get to school and drive the kids home later this afternoon. And I'm the carpool driver this week."

The homeowner, Bea Randolph, looked quizzically at Kate, but recognized her distress. Kate explained the situation as best she could in a short few sentences, but before she could finish, the shocked and sympathetic Bea hesitantly started to talk to Kate. "Mrs. Parker, I mean Kate, you know this is a small enclave we both live in. Everybody has secrets they don't share. For thirty years, my husband, Colonel Randolph, had a drinking problem. Oh, to the outside world, he was a commanding presence. In the house, with me, he was a bully, too. A few glasses of scotch were all he needed to start his tirades against me and the whole world. He never got physically violent, but his harangues could last for hours. In his drunken mind, I was a lousy housekeeper and hostess to his army buddies. He blamed me for not giving him sons to follow him in the military. Our one daughter stopped talking to him entirely. She and I had to meet surreptitiously until she moved out West with her own family. Without a war to fight, he was miserable, taking his frustration out on me. One day, I felt he was taking the life out of me. I went to talk to my pastor who told me Christian marriage was forever. I couldn't deal with that. My daughter and I spoke often by phone. Laura told me, 'One big cut hurts less than a thousand little cuts.' That's when I knew Dave had to leave, forever.

"I was lucky, I guess. He did leave. Joined the Air National Guard out in South Hampton. He was in his element, giving orders again to the pilots who flew each month.

"Kate take a rest for yourself. Come back here later this

afternoon, I'll be ready to leave whenever you get here, and we'll do the carpool together."

Crying softly, Kate was both ashamed and grateful. "Thank you. Thank you. You saved my life."

Back at home, Kate felt compelled to give her mother a call. Ostensibly, it would be to truly thank her for being there for her, for helping her keep some sanity. Somehow, she would bring the conversation around to, hopefully, get some insight into her mother's usual dealings with her.

Kate turned off the TV, sat down at the coffee table in the living room, and picked up her cell phone. "Hi, Mom. I just wanted to call and see how you're doing."

"Oh, I'm doing as well as can be expected. I haven't seen or heard from *you* for a while, or the boys."

"Sorry, Mom. there's been a lot going on. I didn't want to call with my troubles and make you feel bad."

"How *should* I feel? How does a mother feel when her daughter swallows pills and nearly kills herself in the process? You've always needed rescuing, Kate. In school, you always complained about the unfair teachers who demanded too much of you. You and Jane, with her nervous stomach, always in the school bathroom throwing up. Me having to make endless trips to the principal for one thing or another.

Boredom had colored Alice's marriage and damaged her relationship with two of her daughters. Only Rose had escaped their mother's hostility. Rose had been the strong daughter. Kate thought of something Patsy had said in therapy one session: "We are all victims of victims."

"Mom, I am so sorry you had to go through all that pain, carrying the burden of your miserable childhood."

"Well, somebody had to be the strong one in the family. It certainly wasn't your father! He's a dreamer—a successful one, but a dreamer all the same. Rose always knew her mind and went after what she wanted with resolve. I never had to worry about her."

"Yes, but there was Jane and me, especially me, especially after last year. I'm so sorry, Mom, for everything."

"It is what it is, Kate."

"Mom, I just want you to know I am working on myself. I just know things are going to improve. I'm getting stronger. I'm in therapy. I have a good lawyer. Eric will not destroy me. You'll see."

Alice sighed in resignation.

Drained from the conversation, Kate felt she needed the rest Bea Randolph had suggested she take.

She set her phone alarm and woke three hours later. She let Winnie outside to do her doggie business, took a shower, dressed, and began the walk up the road to Bea's house.

Having Bea's company made the carpool drive go easier on Kate's nerves. It had been an emotional morning. Kate's thoughts went back to her conversation with her mother. She was glad Bea was driving.

Late that afternoon, Kate's car mysteriously re-appeared in her driveway. She spent an hour putting away the groceries—tossing mushy "frozen" foods, limp produce, warm meats—cursing Eric the whole time.

Eric's laughing voice on the phone that evening let her know she had no power to stop him from entering his house and taking what he jointly owned.

That night Kate lay in bed, tormented by thoughts of what else Eric could come up with. Would he hold up the support check, not take the children on weekends, breach the sanctuary of her home again?

Chapter

Twenty Four

With each passing week, rage boiled more strongly within Kate. "I have to stop this torture, and soon," she told Maddie as they walked along the trail near their houses. "Nobody will believe what I've been through, and I have no proof of the crazy things he's doing to me. I just want to be through with this marriage and live my life in peace. "I'm going to go to where Eric lives and give him a taste of what he does to me," Kate said to Maddie.

Maddie did her utmost to convince Kate to take the high road, let it be.

Kate woke up Saturday morning, dreading Eric's arrival later that morning. He'd promised the boys a special outing, and they were looking forward to it. Kate got up and fixed the coffee. She sat down on the couch and picked up a book, trying as best she could to take her mind off Eric and the day ahead.

At nine, she woke the boys and got them moving. She had

helped them pack the night before. Kate told the boys to bring their bags downstairs while she finished preparing their breakfast. They ate and talked and waited for the doorbell to ring.

The wait continued, and the boys grew restless.

"When's he going to get here, Mom? Can you just call him? Why's he so late?" Josh asked the same questions again and again. "We're going to be late for the boat if he doesn't get here soon."

Kate finally snapped. "I'm not the one at fault here, Josh!" She sent the boys outside to play. Everything was ready for this day to start, except for Eric. Kate, tired of being the victim, decided to take the situation into her own hands.

She told the boys the plans with their dad were canceled. Then she called around and arranged play dates for them.

After dropping them off at their friends' houses, with a lame excuse about having forgotten a doctor's appointment, Kate made the forty-minute drive to Eric's rental in Hampton Bays.

She banged repeatedly on his door, yelling for him to come out and face her like a man.

The door opened. Eric stood there—grinning—a twelve-gauge shotgun in his hands.

"This is how I kill sharks on our boat. You're on my property. Get out of here. Now."

Kate could see Heather's open mouth. The door slammed. Kate stood for a few seconds listening to the loud laughs coming from inside before returning to her car and heading home.

After that, Kate became determined to put an end to her pain. She was surer now that he enjoyed this game of cat and mouse, and had no intention of stopping. But she was no longer playing the mouse.

Chapter

Twenty Five

The day was warm and bright, with a soft breeze coming off the ocean, a lovely summer's day. Kate was still in an agitated state of mind. She decided to turn on the TV to a women's talk show. Two of the panel members were in a heated argument. One woman was about Kate's age. The other was a short-tempered, controlling, older woman who reminded Kate of her own mother. Kate sat down, watching the contentious interaction between the two women. She wondered why her mother seemed so hostile much of their lives together.

Her dad had been a great businessman and provider, yet a gentle soul. Mother had an easy life, as Kate recalled it. Yet she had always been tough for Kate to deal with. Kate knew they had things to work out between them. It was a puzzlement to her. Being in therapy had Kate questioning her own life and motivations.

The next six weeks flew by. Kate was comfortable with Jake. They took in movies, went out for ice cream, went to local productions, laughed a lot, shared prior dating stories. The passion was real and often. Satisfying.

Jake invited her to his home for the first time. He prepared a real seduction dinner—prime rib, Duchesse potatoes, beautifully-dressed salad, two excellent bottles of vintage Bordeaux. They passed on dessert. Upstairs to Jake's bedroom, dropping clothes and ready for ecstatic sex.

June's luscious warmth greeted Kate, the ripeness of summer in the air.

Some weekends, Jake had his young daughter staying with him. At first, neither one of the lovers had met the other one's children. When they finally got together, the boys and Lily played as if they'd all been friends forever.

Lately, however, Kate had felt a kind of discomfort when Jake returned from handing his daughter back to her mother . . . he seemed distant, preoccupied.

One Sunday afternoon, as they were taking a walk along the local beach, seagulls looking for clams cawed overhead, the sun warm on their faces, Jake turned to Kate. His brow looked creased. His expression was troubled. *What was its cause?*

Jake dropped Kate's hand. "Kate, I've been hearing a lot of nasty stuff about your husband."

"My soon-to-be ex-husband, you mean."

"He's become the talk of the town, screwing every woman he can get his hands on. He even had an ongoing affair with the physics department secretary, I'm told. Didn't you know about any or all of this disgusting stuff while you two were living together? It would seem anyone with any insight into a working marriage would have picked up the clues a long time ago."

"How do you know about all of this, Jake? How long has it been roiling around inside of you? You seem to be accusing me of being either a dummy or else playing at marriage for the perks of remaining Mrs. Physics Professor."

"Listen, Kate, you know how small this community is. It just happens one of my clients has a pending lawsuit against the university physics department for falsifying a patent result. He's seen you and me together, and he thought I ought to know what nasty situation could evolve from our dating.

"He clued me in about Eric. How vicious his temper gets whenever he is under fire for even some minor imagined disrespect he senses about his research."

Kate's reaction was to ask Jake what the conversation was leading up to. Her heart seemed to shrink within her.

"Marion, my ex, is afraid Eric might try some sort of retribution if he thinks I'm getting too close to his kids. She's worried about Lily and is afraid for me as well. Eric sounds so volatile, he might even be jealous of you dating someone seriously."

Kate took a deep breath. "Our kids have been hitting it off so well since we got them together. But that doesn't impact Eric. His issues are with me and our marriage. I seriously doubt Eric would harm either you or Lily."

Jake stopped walking, took hold of Kate's hands, then let them drop. "Kate, I just can't take the chance. I am so sorry it's worked out like this."

Kate stood immobile. She remembered crying in the past, wondering how any man would want to get close to her with her crazy former husband in the picture. Now the reality of her fears had come to life.

Before she could gain control of her emotions, she began to shake. Her face felt wet and hot. Tears wouldn't stop. Jake put his arms around her, trying to comfort Kate. Silently they walked back to his car, passing the happy young children swinging in the playground near the beach snack shack.

Kate looked deeply into Jake's soft eyes and gentle face. Jake was the solid man she knew she needed in her life. He reminded her of her favorite movie actor of all time, James Garner. Breezily handsome, reliable, funny, and smart. All in one package. She had the feeling this was the man for her. She would not cave in to regret just now. Sad as she felt, Kate managed a smile. "I understand your feelings, Jake. I respect that you want to protect your daughter. I don't want to put pressure on you."

Jake laughed and nodded his head in agreement. "You're really one terrific woman, Kate. I know I'm going to miss you. I just wish we could go on . . ."

Kate bent down to pick up some sea glass and a few small shells that the tide had deposited on the arm sand.

She pointed to the snack bar. "How about we have an ice cream before we say goodbye." She managed a quick smile for Jake.

They headed toward the snack bar.

After they'd kissed and said their goodbye, Kate drove in silence for the half mile back to her house. Her troubled mind remembered her favorite quote of T. S. Eliot's: "This is the way the world ends. Not with a bang, but a whimper."

Chapter

Twenty Six

The doorbell rang at six o'clock. Kate heard Heather's car door slam. Heather dropped the boys off and sped away. Willing her body to move to the front door to greet her sons, Kate hoped they would not notice her puffy eyes or distracted gaze. She hugged them both to her.

"Mommy, we're starving," Ryan said. "Daddy and Heather left us alone in a movie place watching *Toy Story* while they went to look at condos. It was scary. All we each had to eat was a bag of popcorn and a package of Reese's Peanut Butter Cups. We got water from the water fountain."

Kate had not prepared any supper because she was so used to going out with Jake for meals on weekends. Kate told the boys she was sorry. "I'll look in the kitchen and see what I can rustle up quickly."

She had some leftover chicken curry and rice from Taste of Jaipur's Saturday night take-out meal. They weren't interested. Besides the staples, her pantry contained a couple of cans of tuna, some English muffins, and a jar of olives. A lone bottle of San Pellegrino and a half-filled bottle of orange juice were on a shelf in the fridge next to a carton of eggs. Kate suggested scrambled eggs on toasted English muffins. Ryan and Josh whined, then agreed and quieted down.

They finished eating and started up the stairs. "Boys, put your dirty clothes in the hamper and get ready for your showers." Kate gave a small shudder as she realized tomorrow was day camp's talent show. A thirty-minute drive to Smithtown, followed at three o'clock by fifty youngsters singing off-key, parents *oohing* and *ahhing* over the handicrafts made by their kids. All this in the boiling hot June sun for hours . . . then the drive home in after-work traffic on the main road. *Just kill me now!*

Kate heard the boys' laughter in the shower. She monitored as Josh and Ryan got dried off, grabbed their iPads, put on headphones. For the next hour the house was quiet. Finally, having exhausted themselves, it was bedtime for them.

Kate thought about calling Liz, but decided her energy was done for the day. The phone rang. Hoping it was Jake, feeling regretful, made her run to the living room, plop down on the sofa again, and pick up the call.

"Hi, Kate, it's Maddie. I know it's kind of late to be calling on a Sunday night, but Friday is Harris's fiftieth birthday. He doesn't want any kind of fancy hullabaloo, so I decided why not have a barbecue for just our dearest friends and family. You and I can play catch up. It's been way too long. Harris said he waved hello to you while you were walking Winnie. He said you looked terrific. I'm so glad! I guess things must have quieted down between you and Eric. All to the good. My mother always says, 'Forgive everybody everything.' Certainly, that was Jesus's message on the Cross."

Kate sighed. "And St. Paul said: 'love never dies.'"

"Well, then, why are you always mocking religion then, Kate."

"Maddie, you're a really sweet person, and I know you mean well. I'll have to get back to you about Friday. I have tentative plans to visit my family upstate. We haven't seen each other since Thanksgiving. But I haven't confirmed yet. I do have exciting news to share with you though." Kate's tone softened. "Maybe we can go for one of our walks early in the week."

"That's a great idea. I'll call you tomorrow to set that up."

"I appreciate your thinking of me, Maddie."

"Oh wait, Kate, I nearly forgot. Our church is having a marvelous speaker at our monthly luncheon on Wednesday. Pastor Nelson is speaking on St Paul's Letter to the Corinthians. He always has the best insights into spiritual and marital relations. He helped Harris and me so much. You know, after our troubles." Maddie was nothing if not persistent.

"I'll talk to you in a day or so, Maddie," Kate said before ending the call.

In between watching the talent show and returning back home, Kate managed to fit in a call to Liz.

Liz took the breakup between Kate and Jake in a sorrowful way. "It all seemed so great for so long. I thought Jake had more spine than it would seem. I know how he adores Lily. Anything or anyone who might want to harm her would definitely impact Jake—even to the point of giving up on the most fabulous woman I know.

"Jake's ex-wife wanted him back for a long time, but she cheated on him. I must say in the guy's defense, he is totally over her. I know you're overbooked every day, but how about I come over tomorrow night? Say seven-ish? You don't have to put on a happy face for me, Kate. Just have some booze at the ready is all I ask."

Kate gave a sad little laugh. "Sure, Liz. Tomorrow about seven."

Kate walked slowly upstairs, plopped herself down on her unmade bed. She hadn't had the energy to make it up or do the dishes. Kate could not stop thinking about Jake. She picked through her music, shuffling through the melancholy tracks. Kate put some Ahava bath salts in the bathtub and ran hot water in the tub until it reached the top.

She waited for her tense muscles to relax in the bath salts. Twenty minutes later, she realized with a start that she had fallen asleep in the tub. Kate got out of the tub and grabbed her white terry cloth robe, another reminder of Jake—the wonderful weekend this summer she and Jake had spent at Gurney's Inn in Montauk.

Wrapping her robe tightly around her, Kate remembered Jake's strong arms. God, how she missed him . . .

Next morning, arriving back home after dropping the kids off at day camp, Kate got out of her car, raced to the front door, slammed it behind her. Kate's despair, anger, and deep frustrations boiled over. Here it was summer, her favorite time. Her forty-fourth birthday was only days away. She *ought* to be happy.

Chapter

Twenty Seven

Kate returned from a morning walk and checked her phone. She had taken to walking with either Maddie or Bea most mornings, leaving her phone off and spending time in conversation. Bea and Kate had walked their dogs to the beach several times since the awful occasion of Kate's frantic knock on her door. Kate liked the older woman. Bea had a gentle, comforting way about her. That was something Kate had sorely missed in her own mother. Bea had courage as well. She had survived a hellish, lengthy marriage, yet had found ways to be happy. She taught adult literacy classes at the local library, drove for Meals on Wheels each Thursday, and volunteered at hospice one day a week. She enjoyed a loving relationship with her daughter and three grandchildren. Bea had an air of contentment that Kate found inspiring. Maybe the feminists had something right. *Maybe a woman without a man is like a fish without a bicycle.*

"I think I'm just about through with men . . . Look at yourself, Kate," she shouted to the empty room. "Now you're even talking out loud to yourself!"

Kate flung her body onto the sofa, cell phone in hand. She had missed three phone calls from Rose. Although they hadn't seen each other for some time, Rose and Kate spoke on the phone several times a week. Rational Rose always had a calming effect on Kate. Sometimes she sensed Rose still worried she might do something to harm herself. If anything, that meant more frequent phone calls from Rose. They had become very close though their conversations mostly revolved around shared recipes, getting gray hairs, discussing the kids.

"I can't take much more of this constant despair, aggravation, and anxiety, Rose. Crazy ex-husbands, worried boyfriends . . . You're so lucky to have Don."

Rose answered sharply, "You know, Kate, that's a joke." Rose's voice sounded strained. "Remember when Don said he was going to the lake to go fishing with Martin and the guys for a few days? He told me not to call him, he'd call me, and I believed him. Well, I got an anonymous call. It was a strange man's voice. 'You better tell your fucking husband to leave my wife alone, or I'll re-arrange his face for him.'

"At first I thought he'd called the wrong number. Then my mind went back to all the nights Don's been complaining about all the work he has on his plate, and how he needs to stay late for another consultation. Or else he tells me there was an accident or construction on the highway and that was why he was late." Rose paused to catch her breath.

"Oh, Rose, I am so sorry. I'm so self-absorbed that I never considered you might be having marital problems too. What is it with these guys and their midlife crises? What do you think you'll do?"

"I've just done it. I confronted him last night. I was burning up while he tried to talk his way out by denying everything. Finally, he had nowhere to go with his lies. My memory is much better than his. He's been seeing this young married chick who came in for a consultation last year. And it's serious. I threw Don out last night! He can have his little whore. I'm done."

"Oh, Rose, I feel sick hearing what you've been going through. I'm just in shock. When will you tell the kids?"

"I already did. At least I told Erin. She threatened to run away. Funny isn't it?" Rose said with sarcasm in her voice. "You know someone for half your life. You trust him with your life, and then you find out that you really don't know him at all. I got married to someone I loved, and to get away from our bossy mother. You got married to someone you loved, and to have a 'big life' away from home. We both married such opposites, or so we thought, and yet here we are. What a mess! But I'll be all right. And you will be too. By the way, I'm still coming down for your birthday. We can have a great time commiserating with each other."

"Rose, I, I don't know what to say."

"Kate, honey, what is, is. Right now, I'm just on autopilot."

Over the phone, Kate could hear Rose lighting a cigarette. This was something new. "Now the bastard has you smoking, Rose? I should have guessed something was up in your life. Some sister I am, eh?"

That evening, Kate's phone rang. Her mother's voice, at the highest pitch Kate had ever heard, made her ears hurt. "Did you know about this? I can't believe Rose is being so rash. Has she gone crazy? I can understand you throwing Eric out, that horrible man you married, but Don? This is just terrible. Now I'll have three divorced daughters!"

"Just think, Mom, all our divorces are nothing compared to those Hollywood bimbos that get married, divorced, and remarried within weeks."

"You think this is funny, Kate? I'm sick just thinking about Rose and Don breaking up. What's wrong with you girls? Daddy and I have been married for nearly fifty years. You think it's all been a bed of roses? Unlike you girls, I know how to handle my husband."

"'Handle him?' Dad is the gentlest soul I've ever known. Besides, I don't want to have to 'handle' the man I love."

"Aunt Jeanette always said that Daddy loved me more than he loved his children," her mother replied smugly.

Kate responded, "Why don't you put that on his tombstone when he goes? 'He loved me most.' Or maybe you should put it on yours, too."

"Oh, I can't talk to you any longer, Kate. You're as bad as your sister, and aggravating me even more." The phone went dead.

Who cares, thought Kate as she turned off the phone and threw it onto the couch.

Rose drove down in a rental car, while hers was being repaired, to spend Kate's forty-fourth birthday with her.

They ate a mostly silent dinner at the local beach club restaurant, sharing appetizers, while Rose chain-smoked every chance she got. Later, they went to see one of the worst movies ever, starring an aging Jennifer Aniston in one of her cutesy comedic roles. At one o'clock, they hugged each other goodnight at the guest room door.

"You're amazing, Rose. I love you so much for coming."

When Kate got up late the next morning, Rose was having another cigarette and smiling broadly.

"You look chipper this morning. What's up, Rose?" Kate asked.

"Don just called. He's coming down and wants to move back home. But tonight he wants to take both of us out for your birthday."

Kate felt alternately shocked and sad. Then, trying to be happy for her sister, Kate said, "I'm so glad one of us is going to have a happy ending here."

A couple of hours later, Don breezed in carrying two bouquets of roses. "Happy birthday, Kate, my favorite sister-in-law." He kissed her on the cheek and turned to Rose. "Honey, I've missed you so." He and Rose embraced and kissed. "I've made reservations for the three of us at Herb's—best lobster in the Hamptons."

Although confused, Kate saw Rose return the love shining from Don's eyes. She left them alone to talk, not hearing what they said but noticing how he spoke and behaved sincerely remorseful, humbled even.

That evening, Kate followed her sister's lead, putting on lipstick, grabbing her wrap. Soon all three of them were happy and laughing as they got into Don's Jaguar for the drive to Herb's. The evening couldn't have been better.

The next day everyone talked about the quality of the night as Don put Rose's overnight bag into his car.

"Rose," Kate said before they drove off, "thanks for being there for me this weekend. I'm sorry to leave so early this morning. We just want to get back home and be together."

"Don't be silly, Rosie," said Kate, using the nickname she hadn't used for Rose in many years. "You were a doll to come down to be with me at all! And I'm happy you were able to save your marriage. I really understand. It's all I ever wanted for me and Eric for the longest time."

Chapter

Twenty Eight

A week later, Rose called Kate. She spoke in soft-voiced despair to say Don had moved out again. This time for good.
Kate thought T.S. Eliot got it right when he wrote the
ending to his poem *The Hollow Men*. Yet again, it ended with a
whimper.

Suddenly, summer was over. An early autumn rolled in. By
now, Kate's lawyer had drawn up papers restricting Eric's visits to
weekends when the boys wanted to go with him. She felt humiliat-
ed, living in a small elite town, yet having to have a local cop show
up at her door with Eric, show the cop the legal papers, and stand
by as he asked Ryan and Josh if they wanted to go with their father
for the weekend. But he had brought it on himself.

The look of hatred for Kate on Eric's face as he waited in the
dim background for the boys' answer was unmistakable. It told
Kate their war was not over. In his arrogant way, anyone could tell
who he thought would win this war.

On the weekends, when Josh and Ryan left with their father,

Kate would sit and cry just to relieve the tension in a way she was unable to do in front of the boys.

Just knowing how crazy he could be again, Kate wondered how she would ever find a man who would put up with her mad ex-husband always in the background. Would she have to spend the rest of her life alone?

Late one night, after having just tucked the boys into bed, Kate heard her phone ring. By the time she got to it, the call had gone to voicemail. Eric's voice announced he was coming over to talk.

"Maybe he's tired of all the game playing. Or else he wants to come back home and start over," Kate said to Rose on the phone. "I wish I knew what's up with him."

Eric breezed in and plopped himself down on the sofa. Kate decided to sit there and shut up, let him talk so there'd be nothing he could beat her over the head with.

"Listen, I'm going away again on Joe's sailboat for a couple of weeks. I won't be seeing the boys for a while. I got myself in a jam, and I need time to work it out."

"Work what out?"

"The remnants of my fling with Cathy Andrews, the department secretary. She got knocked up. I don't know if it was mine or her husband's. She's been married for nine years, and no kids. I paid for her to get an abortion. She took it all hard when I told her it was over between us. She turned out to be a whiny bitch and a not very good loser. I told her I'd get her another position in a different department, but she only wants me. What a royal pain in the ass."

Kate felt hope returning, a chance to get on with her life and plans. His admissions played right into her plan for money for the kids. Otherwise, she would tell him of going to Professor Simmons with the sleazy tale of his prize professor and the secretary. Goodbye Professor Eric Parker's big academic career and reputation.

"When do you leave on your trip, Eric?"

"I'm meeting Joe at the boatyard after I leave here." Kate played nice for a little longer, then showed him to the door.

His news gave Kate just what she needed: time. She had him. She contained her glee, but inside she was surging with it. Eric had always thought himself so goddamn smart. That very arrogance blinded him. Even with his brilliance, the morals clause was the one thing in Eric's tenure appointment that might get him fired. If only, if only, his abortive fling with the department secretary could become a reality.

After he left, Kate made herself a stiff vodka and tonic to steady her nerves. Nothing. She gulped down another with a big slice of lime, then reached for the phone book in the kitchen drawer: *Andrews, Matthew and Cathy.*

Kate picked up the phone and carried it into her bedroom. She lay down on the bed and dialed. Matthew Andrews' voice answered her call.

"Mr. Andrews, your wife is a whore."

"Who is this?"

"The wife of the man Cathy's been fucking."

"You're drunk," he said and hung up on Kate.

Kate felt relaxed for the first time in what seemed like forever. She laughed out loud. "Forget suicide," she giggled. "Revenge is so much more satisfying."

In the meantime, Kate knew she had really had it with group therapy. Things seemed to be heading like a speedball toward the climax of her ending with Eric. She needed to wrap up her stay in the cocoon. Her nerves could no longer take the endless sessions. She knew, to be fair, that everyone was fed up with her ongoing soap opera. She felt calm about it.

Next Thursday she would say her goodbyes. Group had provided a safety valve on her pressure-cooker life experiences with Eric. Kate called Vinnie on Monday to let him know in advance of her decision to leave the group sessions.

"Kate, I have to admit you've done some great work on yourself since you joined the group. You came in as if you were going to the guillotine, yet you faced your antipathy and made the group face its own problematic interactions and dilemmas. I feel you can let go now and be okay with yourself and your decisions. Just remember what I once told you in our early one-on-one sessions: 'No matter what happens, my feet will hold me up.'"

Vinnie had given her a hard push, but she hadn't fallen. She shook her head, smiled, as she recalled how surprised she'd been when Vinnie did that in his office. It seemed like forever ago. She'd felt so weakened by Eric's onslaughts, had been such a lost soul.

Thursday, Kate dressed for her final meetup with the group. She rehearsed how she could best put it to the little ensemble they'd become, without seeming to negate the experience or make herself seem "above" therapy and dismissive of each one of them. Kate did her makeup, then took a good look at herself in the bathroom mirror. She hesitated, feeling a pang in her throat. Patsy and Jess she would miss the most. But it was time to let go. They would be all right. They could always talk on the phone and meet up outside of group.

On with her AG jeans and light blue cashmere sweater that felt like a comforting old friend. She grabbed her keys and cell, flinging them into her denim shoulder bag.

The front doorbell chimed. Robin was there a few minutes early, as usual, to sit for the boys. "There's pizza on the kitchen counter: one plain and one with everything. The boys can have soda tonight as a special treat."

With that, Kate said her goodbyes to Robin, calling out good night to Josh and Ryan. *Did they even hear? Oh, those electronics!*

She started down the driveway. The car's response seemed sluggish, reminding herself to make an appointment with the garage for a long overdue tune-up.

Kate was the first of the group to arrive at Vinnie's office. She paced around and around, getting her thoughts together. Patsy came in next, giving Kate a hug. Her partner in crime had a huge grin on her face. She plopped down on the sofa, letting out a sigh. Soon, like actors in a long-running repertory ensemble, everyone was in place ready for the night's action, or maybe inaction.

Kate couldn't contain her thoughts and anxiety. She leaned forward and looked at each of the familiar faces in the room. She felt very warm. Sentences rushed out of her mouth like a waterfall.

"Listen. I don't know how else to say this, but to tell you straight out, this is my last night in group. I've learned so much from all of you. Sometimes, I don't know how you were able to stand my constant bellyaching, tears, and outright discombobulation. And I have to admit, I wanted to run out of this place more times than I can say. I've wanted to tear my hair out many times with some of your shit, too."

She looked around and saw the frowns. "But, it was never an option to quit on any of our part. We stuck it out together."

Joe had a scowl on his face. Nothing new there. Sarcastic as ever, he said, "We ever had a choice? Your pissing and moaning made me feel a lot like Eric must have lots of times. You gals expect, no *demand*, us guys to jump higher and higher. He screws around some and gets the shaft. But there's just no satisfying you. You get the kids, the house, the prestige."

"Joe, will you never *not* be an asshole?" That was Patsy's reply. "We have the right to ditch morons like my ex or torturers like Eric. It's either that or become a cringing little woman or junkie or something."

"I agree, Patsy. I was lucky with Steve. Since the rape, he takes my side, no matter how crazy I get at times. Maybe he's not the most scintillating partner, but we keep growing closer."

"Yeah, tell yourself that. Whatever makes your world go around. I'll never get women."

"Look, Joe," Pete broke in, "even though my ex was a drunk, I'm still in the game. Michelle and I've been dating for seven months now. I'm getting my confidence in women back. I trust her with my feelings. Too bad you've let your bitterness overrule your life."

Vinnie turned to Rhoda and Eden. His eyes rested on each of them. Eden had her head lowered. When she looked up, tears were in her eyes. She shook her head, unwilling or not able to express what she was feeling. Rhoda's words were of some comfort to Kate.

"Kate, I know how you've struggled to come to grips with Eric. You're a good person, a good mother, and I know God will answer your prayers and give you inner peace. It's what we all want and need: Grace. God's Grace."

"Amen to that," added Dan. He got up and walked over to

Kate. He put his arms around her and turned to Vinnie. "It's Kate's last time with us, Vinnie. I just had to give her a hug."

"Okay. We can have a final group hug. That is, Joe, if you don't mind!"

"What the hell do I care?"

So, it was done. Trailed to her car by Patsy and Jess, Kate leaned on the car door. She was exhausted. Another ending.

Chapter

Twenty Nine

Life can be so unpredictable. All bets suddenly were off, because two weeks later, Eric was back in New York.

Eric had returned from his crisis boat trip looking tanned and acting smug, as usual, toying with and giving orders to Kate, as before.

He told Kate he was taking only Ryan with him for the weekend. They were going fishing out East with one of his male friends. Josh always got seasick, so he would have to stay home with Kate. Eric told her he would come by for Ryan at eleven o'clock on Sunday morning.

Kate was looking forward to having her sweet son to herself. She thought they could walk to the beach and eat hot dogs. She could push him on the swings and hunt for seashells with him. It was too cold for swimming, but they would have fun together.

Chapter

Thirty

At five o'clock Sunday evening, a knock came at the door.
It was a female officer. "Mrs. Parker, I'm afraid I have
some bad news for you."

Kate's heart began beating hard. She couldn't stop the pounding in her chest.

"There's been an accident. A rogue wave hit the Shinnecock Inlet and your husband's boat capsized. He and his friend, Mr. Peterson, were thrown clear, but your son was sleeping in a cabin downstairs. The men had been sand shark hunting with twelve-gauge shotguns, and your son had been fishing. He got tired and went to take a nap downstairs."

"Oh my God. Oh no. Not Ryan." She wanted to die, to kill herself for real this time, certain it was her punishment for planning revenge on Eric for her own gain. *No revenge against Eric. Just heartbreak for me.*

"According to Mr. Peterson, your husband was an excellent diver. He kept diving down to try to free Ryan as the cabin was filling up with water. He managed to finally break open a window and drag the boy out to the surface, which is where we found them all. Unfortunately, I'm sorry, but . . . "

Kate was losing it. Her feet were buckling under her. She was afraid she might faint.

"We got him to shore, but he collapsed and died, an apparent heart attack. The strain was too much for Dr. Parker's heart. I'm very sorry, Mrs. Parker, I have to tell you, the paramedics did everything they could, but they couldn't revive him. It's so rare in a man as young as your husband . . . "

Kate's head was throbbing, her stomach turning. She couldn't focus, could barely hear his words.

"Did you understand what I said? We need you to drive out to pick up your son and arrange for your husband's body. I know it isn't much comfort, but you'll always have the satisfaction of knowing how much your husband loved his son."

"Yes, yes, of course. Yes, I need to go get my son," Kate said. Ryan would be terrified, traumatized. He would need Kate's tenderness, and her strength.

"Survival is everything," Kate said to no one. Eric would have appreciated the irony. *A boating accident and my marriage problems are solved forever. Eric, so controlled and controlling, gets done in by a rogue wave on a sunny Saturday.* It was too ironic for words. Kate knew it would be all right now. With Eric's insurance payout and retirement fund, her turn at living was at hand.

"Thank you, officer. Is there anything else?"

"We need you to identify the body."

"Right now? I need be here for my son, for both of my sons. I need to pick up Ryan."

"Yes, of course, ma'am." The officer handed her card to Kate. "And ma'am, we have a hotline you can call for grief counseling. You're probably in shock. Anyone would be with a tragedy like this."

Kate told the officer she would need time to sort out her options and how best to help her boys come out of this in the healthiest way. She thanked the officer once more and went back inside the house. Kate felt baffled by her mixed emotions. She began to think back on the happy times when she and Eric first met and fell for each other.

How did life get so screwed up with lies and betrayal? Such a frigid end to their hot love story.

She was no Scarlett O'Hara. No putting this off till another day. Kate would have to get through Eric's funeral, put on widow's weeds, and behave somberly. She had survived all that had been thrown at her. Her dreams, which had been submerged for what seemed like forever, were free to rise to the surface. She could handle what came her way, but first some other things had to be done. Consoling Josh came first, though in truth it would take a lifetime.

Kate called Bea for a ride to pick up Ryan. She called Robin to sit with the boys for a few hours, and she called Liz to drive her to the morgue.

Chapter

Thirty One

After a few minutes of talking and crying with Liz, Kate hung up the phone. She went upstairs to check on Josh again.

Kate walked into Ryan's room to pack him some fresh clothes and gather a few items that might bring him some comfort. He was going to need plenty of comfort, and plenty of her time and attention for the next several months. She sat down on his bed, spent a few minutes feeling immense gratitude for Ryan's safety. Standing up, Kate straightened Ryan's bedding and wiped away a tear, taking in some reviving breaths of freedom.

Strangely, the one person she most wanted to talk to was her mother.

Her mother's first words were startling. "I don't know how you stood that man for so long. Losing Eric is like losing a bad case of the flu. I'm sorry, Kate. I'm just beginning to see that you have always been the strong one in the family. You've been dealing with a soul-crushing man who was as rough as the tide that's taken him away. Now is the real new life you deserve, my precious girl. You have more guts than I've had. I stayed with him to save face, and I avoided living my own life. Sorry to say that to you. You were his favorite daughter, after all. You are stronger than you think. You've raised two wonderful boys—and now you're all going to be fine, Kate."

Kate was speechless. She let the tears come down her pale face. Her mother's words were a gift hoped for but always held back from her. Kate hung up the phone, wiped her eyes with a tissue. She had lived with difficult, demanding, and emotionally stunted men, beginning with her gentle but ultimately put-upon father. But she had survived.

Bea dropped Kate and the boys back at their house. As she stood there on the threshold, her boys' hands in her own, she was overcome with gratitude. Both of her boys were alive. Little by little, she would begin to put together a new life for herself and her sons.

She could recover her sense of competence again. A new role would present itself in time, and she could handle it—no, she could excel at it.

As soon as Robin arrived, Kate got herself ready for Liz's arrival, feeling lucky to have a friend to make the journey with her. Liz would go with her and hold her up. Rose and her parents would be driving to Stony Brook to be with the boys and help with funeral arrangements. Kate could not begin to think of how she would proceed. So untimely. The boys must be comforted and reassured of her love and support. She must be totally there for them.

Liz pulled into the driveway. Time to get moving. She could make more phone calls while Liz drove.

Liz and Kate hugged. Liz went upstairs to comfort the boys while Kate spoke to Robin.

Liz and Kate talked a little as Liz drove toward the shore.

"Liz, do you mind if I call Rose. I need to let her know."

"Of course, honey."

Kate called Rose, who picked up on the first ring. "Mom just called me with the news, Kate. I was about to call you. I feel just terrible. I want to come over and hug you. I'm in shock. Eric was such a bastard, you know. But still, he was your boys' father."

Kate's resolve not to cry melted away with Rose's words. "Rose, I just need time to process it all. I can't talk about any of it right now. Even to you. I'll call you tomorrow after I take Ryan to the doctor and have him checked out. The officer told me Ryan has a lot of puncture wounds from the fishing rod hooks that went into his arms when the boat capsized. He was asleep below deck when the boat flipped. That's my first priority right now. Plans for Eric's funeral will come soon enough."

"Kate, you are one amazing woman. Here you always thought I was the strong one. I can spout off all kinds of advice, but you are doing the living, the nearly unimaginable."

Chapter

Thirty Two

Kate's brain went into shutdown mode. She was beyond thinking, beyond comprehension. She took care of what needed to be done, moving from one decision and task to the next. Dr. Erdogan checked out Ryan's injuries. Fortunately, they were superficial and not infected.

All the trauma, the acrimony, the dangerous interactions with Eric suddenly ended. The news of Eric's death was printed in the local Stony Brook *Three Village Herald*. There was also a short feature that aired on the local TV news at six and ten o'clock. Kate had refused to comment to any reporters. She counted fifteen phone calls from Eric's university colleagues. After another flood of calls from friends, Kate's voice was raspy. She was entirely out of energy.

Drained, flooded with alternate brain messages, she let the phone keep ringing. Every one of the callers wanted to offer condolences and to know about funeral arrangements. If she weren't so exhausted, she'd have screamed or wept.

Along with the shock of Eric's sudden death, depression was

settling in. In her mind, amid their ongoing psychological and physical battles, she had many times wished Eric dead. Now he was gone. Gone—her first love, her sons' father, the brilliant scientist, the respected professor . . . and her tormentor.

The only family she could deal with were her mother and Rose. Her younger sister, Jane, was too emotionally fragile to handle life's ordinary situations and was frightened of anything to do with death. She planned to stay in her parents' home with her young daughter until the funeral. Perhaps, she might not make it for that.

Late the next morning, with the sun shining brightly in the clear blue sky, Kate rubbed her eyes as she stood on the porch, thinking, thinking. Her family was on their way to Stony Brook and would arrive around two o'clock. Together, they would brainstorm what to do in the aftermath of Eric's passing. Kate needed the comfort of their presence and knew they would help her with the difficult choices she'd need to make.

The boys were at Liz's place, with its swimming pool, hot tub, and big-screen TV. Kate could make phone calls and discuss funeral plans without them in earshot.

Liz was great with Josh and Ryan. Not having kids of her own, Liz had a menagerie of animals, a small zoo, in her huge fenced-in backyard. Two miniature horses, a mule, chickens, a pot-bellied pig, a goat, and a one-eyed llama co-existed happily, along with an ancient gray cat and two Golden Retrievers. The boys loved going to visit Aunt Liz. They happily fed the miniature horses and mule apples and carrots. They would sleep over there tonight, nestled in Liz's guest room with the two dogs, one for each of the boys on his own twin bed. Then they'd come home to spend the day with family tomorrow.

At last, Kate was surrounded by tender kisses and the strong arms of her family. These condolences Kate could tolerate. Tears came to her eyes, breaking the grip of numbness she had been experiencing.

Although the refrigerator and counters were full of food, brought over by those who came to offer their sympathy, no one felt hungry. "I'd just like a cup of Earl Grey tea, if you have some," her mother said. Her father lit a cigar and went outside to smoke it. Rose also opted for tea.

"Hot or iced?" Kate managed to ask.

"Iced for me, please," Rose requested.

For Kate, just getting together the few items to serve tea seemed to pass in slow motion. She took a sprig of mint from a small pot on the kitchen counter, added ice cubes, and handed Rose her cool drink.

"Sugar?"

Both her mother and Rose asked for two teaspoons apiece. Kate went blank for a moment.

"I'm sorry. I don't know that I have sugar. I think I used the last of it when I made cookies."

"Kate, honey, don't stress about it," Rose said. "Let's all just go outside and sit at the round table under the sun umbrella and unwind."

Kate persisted, "We have to make a decision soon about Eric. It was so awful going to see his body. I was up all night. I must decide what to do."

"Arranging a funeral by yourself is too much for you, Kate. Besides, a lot of people you'd expect to attend are probably away on summer vacations," her mother coolly answered. "Everyone who can come will be there. They'll come out of respect to you. Besides, not everyone knew the 'real' Eric."

"Oh, Mom, let's not go there right now. I can't. I just can't."

Rose picked up her iced tea, sipping it slowly. Softly, she said, "Probably the easiest thing would be to have a graveside service, with just the immediate family and a few close friends. Then, in September, when school starts up again, you can hold a memorial service at the university chapel if you want to. That will give you time to breathe as well as to go over financials and such. What do you think, Mom?"

"Rose has a point there, Kate. You will have Josh and Ryan back in school, Eric's colleagues will be back from wherever they went for the summer, and you can begin to think of your own future. Yours and the boys'."

"*My* future . . . Josh's and Ryan's future. It's so overwhelming."

"But, Kate, remember you have gotten this far on guts and strength already. Sooner than you think, I know you will be able to do what you both need to do for the boys and yourself. Soon enough, you be able to pursue your own career. Won't that be *marvelous?* I know you can do it!"

"Rose, you always know what to say. I suppose there is that hope."

"Just think how strong you've had to be these last years just to survive Eric's never-ending torments."

From the corner of the garden, Kate's father walked toward the women.

"Listen, to your mother and Rose, Kate. They're making a lot of sense, sweetheart." He tenderly patted Kate's soft hair.

"Dad, I just hope I can bring the boys up to be kind and loving, to be good to their wives."

"You will, my dear. You'll set a fine example of caring and decency for those boys. No doubt about it."

Chapter

Thirty Three

Maddie called Kate to say she would ask her pastor to serve at the memorial. Kate hesitated at first, then thanked Maddie for her kindness in offering to arrange it.

The religious rituals were set. That was the easiest part. But how to ease the boys' suffering with the loss of their father. And how would she cope? There was so much pain to go around. Energy sapped, Kate could feel her shoulders tense, then sag. She thought of Dr. Rossetti now. It would be a healing of sorts to process what Eric's death would men to Josh and Ryan, and herself. Her adversary in life had also been a good father to the boys when he could focus on their needs. Her mind flashed back to the videos of Eric holding the boys in his arms when they were toddlers, teaching them to swim, to ride their bikes. He'd grinned the day each son had been able to ride his bike with its training wheels off for the first time. She recalled his showing them the nighttime sky through the telescope he'd set up in the backyard near the swimming pool. Before the divorce and the endless pain of its aftermath.

Kate and Dr. Rossetti met in his office. She did not wear black. Dr. Rossetti got up from his desk and expressed his condolences. "I know this is an extra rough time for you, Kate. Who ever thought this would be the ending to everything?" He shook his head.

"I am so confused, Dr. Rossetti. How do I process all of this? What do I tell the boys to make it all easier for them? They're so young to lose a parent."

He nodded his head in agreement. "I feel it's best to let them ask all the questions and answer them as truthfully as you feel they can understand at their age. Ryan may take it harder than Josh because he was there when it all happened. He's somewhat young to feel survivor's angst. It may comfort him to know his dad tried to save his life, or he may be awash in guilt. We can work to prevent that from happening. Josh may feel relieved to have been with you at home. Both boys will probably tend to cling to you more for some time. The fear of losing you as well may even bring on nightmares. I would be happy to recommend a very fine pediatric psychiatrist to help the boys deal with their trauma, if you'd like."

"Yes, that would be great. It would be really great to have someone with a caring manner talk with them in a soothing way. A mom, especially this mom, has virtually nothing left in the tank to handle Ryan's and Josh's questions about Eric right now."

"I'm referring you to Dr. Helen Aldrich. I'll call and apprise her of the situation. I'm sure she'll get back to you quickly. She'll want to meet with you first, of course."

Kate stood and nodded. "I understand. Thanks, Dr. Rossetti. We've come nearly full circle now. Goodbye and thanks again."

Chapter

Thirty Four

There would be a service at Maddie's church, with burial to follow at the small cemetery near Conscience Bay. Liz was going to arrange the after-service catering to be held outdoors at Kate's house.

Kate chose September fourteenth for the campus memorial service. This year's Indian Summer meant a warm and sun-filled day. She raised her face to the warmth of the late summer afternoon. Kate mused on how fast time seemed to be going by. Before too long it would be Halloween, then Thanksgiving, and soon after that, Christmas again.

Was it nearly a year since she and Liz had shared those Mai Tais as the first snowflakes were beginning to fall softly? Here she was, Eric's funeral in three days and his memorial soon after. She would need to find the right clothes for the boys and buy a suitable outfit for herself. No widow's weeds, of course. But something appropriate for her indeterminate status.

She asked her mother and father to help the boys with their

outfits. They were honored to do so. Then she called Liz for help with her own.

"Remember, you're aiming for something somber, but youthful," Liz said to Kate as they climbed the escalator of Bloomingdale's, heading to the dress department. "No black anything, no black dress, definitely no veil. No Jackie Kennedy grief here."

"Still, I want to look appropriate, Liz. Eric was a shit all right, but he had sons who saw him differently than we did."

Stopping a salesperson, Kate explained what she was looking for. "Oh, I'm sorry for your loss. This is not the right department. You'll want the suit department. I'm sure you'll find something suitable."

Liz couldn't resist joking. "A suitable suit! Ha ha!" Kate shot her an annoyed look, but on they went to the next floor.

Kate went through the racks of fashionable clothing. Although the weather was very warm, inside the store was already filled with mannequins dressed in fall clothing.

An hour later, Kate walked out with her purchase of a black-and-white hounds-tooth linen blazer, black linen skirt, and black silk short-sleeved blouse. She had black shoes at home in her closet. For the memorial service in the university chapel, Kate decided on a simple black-skirted suit with a white crepe blouse. She was surprised to need both in size four, down from her usual size six. The black pumps would do service again.

She and Liz stopped for lunch in Bloomingdale's before heading home. Kate still had last minute phone calls to make for the memorial service. Family, colleagues, neighbors . . .

"You know, honey, I think you should give Jake a call and invite him to the memorial."

"Are you crazy, Liz? I will not call Jake. That ship has sailed without me."

"Time changes things, Kate. You never know."

Chapter

Thirty Five

The funeral service went off without a hitch. Kate had tossed a handful of dirt on Eric's polished mahogany coffin. She held the hands of her young sons as they bowed their heads in a little prayer for Eric.

His mother's grief showed plainly on her face. To her, Eric was irreplaceable. She and Eric's sister, Victoria, walked over to hug and kiss the boys. His mom gave an anguished look to Kate, who nodded in return. Victoria suggested they'd like to spend more time with the boys, get to know Josh and Ryan. Something Eric hadn't permitted. Kate asked about Eric's father, but they just shook their heads.

Kate noticed Heather at the back of the church, and at the cemetery. They didn't speak, and Kate didn't invite her back home. Fortunately, Cathy Andrews didn't turn up at all.

After the service, the small group departed the cemetery for a tastefully presented buffet at Kate's house, courtesy of Liz. It was four o'clock before the last home guests left.

Kate's parents and Rose were staying at Kate's for ten days to give her some help and time to rest. They wanted to looked after the boys and be there for their first day of school, the Tuesday after Labor Day weekend.

Chapter

Thirty Six

September fourteenth finally arrived. Soon her duties to Eric would be done. Kate could begin to plot out some sort of future for herself. Sometime in October she'd begin to work on updating her resumé for next semester. Whatever path she took, she must be near enough to have quality time with Ryan and Josh, who were seeing Dr. Aldrich once a week for now.

At ten o'clock, the university chapel began filling up, Faculty, students, and friends soon took up all the seats in the tasteful chapel, with its altar wafting fragrance from white lilies, roses, and chrysanthemum arrangements. An organist played simple hymns in the background. Maddie's pastor stood ready to begin the service. Everyone stood up.

Kate glanced behind her at the crowded chapel as people stirred and stood up at their seats. The rear door opened, letting in a shaft of sunshine. She stood in her place, wide-eyed and staring. Framed in the sunlight was Jake. Kate had to blink several times to believe this was not a mirage. Then she nodded and smiled back at Jake's broad grin. Maybe it was inappropriate, but her heart was in charge.

Oh, that Liz! Wait until I get hold of her. Some friend. The greatest!

# # #

About the Author

Aiming for the Heart is Barbara Keating's second work of fiction.

Keating has studied both at the Santa Barbara Center for Lifelong Learning and as a private writing student with several professional writers and editors.

She holds a graduate degree as a clinical social worker specializing in work with emotionally disturbed children and families from Fordham University in Tarrytown, New York.

She currently lives in Santa Barbara, California. Her first novel is *The Second Coming of Carrie Rogers*.

www.ingramcontent.com/pod-product-compliance
Lightning Source LLC
Chambersburg PA
CBHW070939250626
47159CB00009B/3315